KINGFISHER
Larousse Kingfisher Chambers Inc.
95 Madison Avenue
New York, New York 10016

First American edition 1996
2 4 6 8 10 9 7 5 3 1

LIBRARY OF CONGRESS CATALOGING-IN-PUBLICATION DATA

Andersen, H C (Hans Christian), 1805-1875, Tales, English, Selections
A treasury of stories from Hans Christian Andersen [complied by] Jenny Koralek,
illustrated by Robin Lawrie—1st American ed. p. cm.
Summary: Presents retelling of some familiar fairy tales, including "The Emperor's
New Clothes, "The Nightingale,"and "Thumbelina." 1. Fairy tales—Denmark.
2. Children's stories, Danish—translations into English.
[1. Fairy tales, 2. Short stories.] I. Koralek, Jenny. II Lawrie, Robin, [1] III. Title.
PZ8.A542T [F1c]—dc20188895-36161 CIP AC

ISBN 1-85697-676-9

Printed in Great Britain

A · TREASURY · OF
STORIES · FROM
HANS CHRISTIAN
ANDERSEN

RETOLD BY

Jenny Koralek

ILLUSTRATED BY

Robin Lawrie

Kingfisher

NEW YORK

CONTENTS

THE TINDERBOX

A soldier was marching along the high road. One, two! One two! He had his knapsack on his back and his sword at his side, for he was on his way home from the wars. On the way he met a hideous old witch who said, "Good evening, soldier. What a fine sword you have, and what a big knapsack! You're a brave soldier and you deserve to have as much money as you like."

"Thank you!" said the soldier.

"Do you see that big tree?" said the witch, pointing to a tree nearby. "It's quite hollow inside. You must climb to the top, and then you'll see a hole, through which you can let yourself down and get deep into the tree. I'll tie a rope around you so that I can pull you out again when you call me."

"What am I to do down in the tree?" asked the soldier.

"Get money," replied the witch. "Listen to me. When you get right into the tree you will find yourself in a great hall. It is quite well-lit, for more than three hundred lamps are burning there. You will see three doors which you can open with the keys hanging there. Go into the first room and you'll see a huge chest in the middle of the floor. On this chest sits a dog, and he's got a pair of eyes as big as two teacups. But don't worry about that. I'll give you my blue checked apron, and you can spread it out on the floor. Then go up quickly to the dog and put him on my apron. Then open the chest and take as many coins as you like. They are made of copper, but if you prefer silver you must go into the second room. There sits a dog with a pair of eyes as big as mill wheels. But don't worry about that. Put him on my apron and take some of the money. And if you want gold, you can have as much as you can carry if

you go into the third room. The dog that sits on the money-chest there has two eyes as big as round towers. He is a very fierce dog but don't worry. Just put him on my apron and he won't hurt you, then take as much gold out of the chest as you like."

"That's not such a bad idea," said the soldier. "But what am I to give you? For I'm sure you aren't doing this as a favor."

"No," replied the witch, "I don't want a single penny. Just bring me an old tinderbox which my grandmother forgot when she was down there last."

"Then tie the rope around me," cried the soldier, "and give me your apron."

Then he climbed up into the tree and let himself slip down into the hole.

He found himself, just as the witch had said, in the great hall where three hundred lamps were burning.

He opened the first door, and there sat the dog with eyes as big as teacups, staring at him.

"Good dog!" said the soldier, and he put him on the witch's apron and took as many copper coins as his pockets would hold. He then locked the chest, put the dog back on it again, and went into the second room. There sat the dog with eyes as big as mill wheels.

"Good dog!" said the soldier and he put the dog on the witch's apron, and when he saw the silver money in the chest, he threw away all the copper money and filled his pockets and his knapsack with silver only. Then he went into the third room. The dog there really did have eyes as big as round

towers, and they turned around and around in his head like wheels.

"Good dog!" said the soldier, lifting him down to the floor and opening the chest. What a mountain of gold there was in that chest! He would be able to buy a whole town with it and all the toy soldiers, candy, and rocking horses in the whole world. The soldier threw away all the silver coins and instead filled all his pockets, his knapsack, his boots, and his cap with gold, so that he could hardly walk. He put the dog back on the chest, shut the door, and then called up through the tree, "Now pull me up, old witch."

"Have you got the tinderbox?" asked the witch.

"Rats!" exclaimed the soldier. "I had quite forgotten about it." And he went back and fetched it.

The witch pulled him up, with his pockets,

boots, knapsack, and cap full of gold.

"What are you going to do with the tinder-box?" asked the soldier.

"Mind your own business!" snapped the witch. "You've got your money, so just give me the tinderbox."

"No!" said the soldier. "Tell me what you're going to do with it, or I'll cut off your head."

"No!" cried the witch.

So the soldier cut off her head. There she lay in the middle of the road. But the soldier tied up all his money in her apron, put it on his back, put the tinderbox in his pocket, and went straight off to town.

He took the finest rooms at the very best inn and ordered his favorite dishes every day. He went out and bought new boots and fancy clothes. He made many friends and they told him all about the magnificent things in their city and how pretty the king's daughter was.

"How can I get to see her?" asked the soldier.

"Oh you can't!" he was told. " She lives in a great copper castle with a great many walls and towers round about it. No one but the king is allowed to go in and out, because it has been prophesied that she will marry an ordinary soldier, and the king won't hear of it."

All the same, I should like to see her, thought the soldier, but he did not know how to go about it.

For a time he led a merry life, but as he spent a lot of money every day and never earned any, he was soon down to his last two coins. He had to move out of his fine rooms and go and live in a little garret under the roof, and clean his boots for himself, and mend his own clothes. None of his friends came to see him anymore; they said there were too many stairs to climb.

One dark evening, when he no longer had enough money to buy himself a candle, the soldier thought there might be a candle in the tinderbox which he had taken out of the tree for the old witch. He took out the tinderbox and sure enough there was a candle in it, but as soon as he lit it the door flew open and in came the dog who had eyes as big as teacups and said: "What are my lord's commands?"

"Well, blow me down!" said the soldier. "What a marvel this tinderbox is if it can give me anything I

want! Bring me some money," he said to the dog. Whisk! the dog was gone, and whisk! he was back again with a great bag full of coins in his mouth.

The soldier soon found out how amazing the tinderbox was. If he struck it once, in came the dog who sat on the chest of copper money; if he struck it twice, in came the dog who had the silver; and if he struck it three times, in came the dog who had the gold. The soldier moved back into the fine rooms and could afford fine clothes again, and all his friends came to see him because he was rich again.

One night he said to himself, it is very strange that one cannot get to see the princess. They all say she is very beautiful, but what is the use of that if she is always shut up in that copper castle with all those towers? Can I really not get to see her? Where is my tinderbox? So he struck a light, and whisk! in came the dog with eyes as big as teacups.

"It's late, I know," said the soldier, "but I should very much like to see the princess, if only for a moment."

And the dog was off at once, and before the soldier could turn around it was back with the princess. There she sat fast asleep on the dog's back. She was so lovely the soldier could not help kissing her. Then the dog ran back again to the castle with the princess still fast asleep.

But in the morning when the king and queen were drinking tea, the princess told them she had had a strange dream the night before, about a dog and a soldier—that she had ridden on the dog, and been kissed by the soldier.

"A likely story!" said the queen.

All the same, that night she ordered a lady-in-waiting to watch by the princess's bed to see what was going on.

The soldier had a great longing to see the lovely princess again, so the dog came in the night and ran off with her as fast as he could. The lady-in-waiting ran just as fast after him. When she saw them going into a house she drew a big cross with some chalk on the door and went home. When the dog came out with the princess he saw the cross on the door where the soldier lived, so he took a piece of chalk too, and drew crosses on all the doors in the town. And that was very clever of him, because when the king and queen came looking for the soldier's door they could not find it because all the doors had crosses on them.

But the queen was an exceedingly clever woman. She took out her gold scissors, cut out a piece of silk, and made a neat little bag. She filled the bag with flour and cut a tiny little hole in the bag, so that the flour would trickle out all along the way if the dog came for the princess again. The queen tied the little bag to the princess while she was fast asleep and waited to see what would happen.

Sure enough, the dog came again, took the princess on his back, and ran with her to the soldier, who loved her very much and wished he were a prince, so that he could marry her. The dog did not notice the flour trickling out in a steady stream from the castle to the door of the soldier's house, but in the morning the king and queen had no trouble seeing where their daughter had been, and they took the soldier and put him in prison.

There he sat in the dark, knowing that he was to be hanged the very next day, and he had left his tinderbox at the inn. In the morning, through the iron grating of the little window, he could see the people hurrying to the gallows where he was to be hanged. He heard the drums beat and saw the soldiers marching.

He called out to a boy running past. "Hey! Don't be in such a hurry. It can't begin until I come. But if you run to my house and bring me my tinderbox, you shall have four gold coins, but you must hurry!"

The boy badly wanted those four gold coins so he quickly fetched the tinderbox, and soon afterward the soldier was taken away to be hanged.

But just as the rope was being put around his neck, he asked if he could smoke one last pipe. The king agreed to this request, so the soldier took out his tinderbox and struck a light. One! Two! Three! And there suddenly stood all the dogs—the one with eyes as big as teacups, the one with eyes as large as mill wheels and the one whose eyes were as big as round towers.

"Help me now, so that the judges do not hang me!" said the soldier.

And the dogs fell upon the judges and shook them till their teeth rattled. The biggest dog chased the king and queen so far out of town that they

never found their way back. Then suddenly everyone was shouting: "Little soldier, you shall be our king and marry the beautiful princess!"

And so they put the soldier into the king's coach, and all the three dogs ran in front barking joyfully. The princess came out of the copper castle and very happily became queen. The wedding lasted a week, and the three dogs sat at the table too, and their eyes grew bigger than ever at everything they saw.

THE EMPEROR'S NEW CLOTHES

There was once an emperor who loved new clothes. He spent all his money on them and liked nothing better than to drive out every day in his carriage and show them off to everybody. He had a coat for every hour of the day and spent far more time deciding what clothes to wear than looking after his empire.

The great city where he lived was very lively. Strangers arrived there every day. One day two cheats arrived. They said they were weavers and boasted that they could weave the finest cloth anyone could imagine. Not only were their colors and patterns, exceedingly beautiful, they said, but the clothes made from their cloth possessed the wonderful quality of being invisible to anyone who was not fit for his job or who was a complete fool.

They must be wonderful clothes! thought the emperor. If I wore them I would know which men in my empire are not fit for their jobs and see at once who is foolish and who is wise. Yes, I must have some of this cloth immediately!

And he gave the two cheats a large sum of money, so that they could begin work at once. The two cheats set up two looms and pretended to be weaving, but there was nothing at all on their looms.

They boldly asked for the finest silk and the costliest gold thread which they put into their own bags, and worked at the empty looms till late into the night.

I should like to know how far they have got with my cloth, thought the emperor. But he felt rather uneasy when he remembered that those who were not fit for their work could not see it. He was sure, of course, that he had nothing to fear for himself, but all the same, he decided he would rather send someone else first to see how the weavers were getting on.

I will send my honest old minister, thought the emperor. He can judge best how the cloth looks. He's no fool and no one understands his job better than he does.

So the good old minister went into the room where the two cheats sat working at the empty looms.

Heaven help us! thought the old minister, his eyes popping out of his head. I cannot see anything at all! But he did not say this.

The two cheats begged him to come closer and asked if he liked the colors and the pattern. Then they pointed to the empty loom, and the poor old minister stared and stared, but he could see nothing, for there was nothing to see.

Heaven's above! he thought. Am I so stupid? I never thought I was, and I don't want anyone else

to think so! And surely I am fit for my job? No, I better not say that I cannot see the cloth.

"Well?" said one of the weavers. "What do you think?"

"Oh, it's beautiful—beautiful!" said the old minister, peering through his spectacles. "What a wonderful pattern, and what lovely colors! Yes, I shall tell the emperor that I am delighted with it."

"Good!" said the weavers, and they told him the names of the colors, and explained the complicated pattern. The old minister listened carefully so that he would be able to repeat it all to the emperor, which he did.

And now the cheats asked for more money and more silk and gold thread, which they said they needed for weaving. They put it all into their own bags and not a thread was put upon the loom, but they went on working at the empty frames as before.

The emperor soon sent another honest minister to see how the weaving was getting on and if the cloth was nearly ready. Like the first minister he looked and looked, but, as there was nothing to be seen, he could see nothing. And because he too did not want to seem foolish and did not want to lose his job, he praised the cloth which he could not see and rushed off to tell the emperor about the beautiful colors and the charming pattern.

By now, everybody was talking about the marvelous cloth and the emperor decided he must see it for himself while it was still on the loom. He took his two honest ministers with him and went to see the cunning cheats, who were now weaving as fast as they could but without any thread.

"Isn't it beautiful?" said the old ministers, pointing at the empty loom.

What's this? said the emperor to himself. I can't see a thing! But that's terrible! Am I stupid? Am I not fit to be emperor? That would be the most

dreadful thing that could happen to me. But out loud he said, "Oh, it's fabulous, I give it my highest approval." And he nodded and smiled and gazed at the empty loom, for he was certainly not going to say that he saw nothing.

The two ministers said, "Yes, it is fabulous, isn't it?" and begged him to wear these splendid new clothes for the first time at the great procession that was soon to take place.

The night before the procession was to take place, the two cheats stayed up and lit hundreds of candles so that the people could see how hard at work they were completing the emperor's new clothes. They pretended to take the cloth down from the loom; they made cuts in the air with great scissors; they sewed with needles without thread; and at last they said, "Now the clothes are ready!"

The emperor came himself with his noble ministers.

"If your Imperial Majesty will be gracious enough to undress," said the cheats, "then we will help you to put on the new clothes here in front of the great mirror."

The emperor took off his clothes, and the cheats pretended to put each new garment on him as it was ready. The emperor turned around and around before the mirror.

"Just look at those trousers!" cried the cheats, "and the coat! and the cloak! Why the cloth is as light as a spider's web. You really would think you had nothing on!"

"Yes!" said the emperor. "They do look good! And how well they fit!"

"They are waiting outside with the canopy which is to be carried above your Majesty in the procession!" said the cheats, who planned to leave town once the procession was under way.

"Well, I am ready," replied the emperor. And then he turned again to the mirror, for he wanted it to look as if he was admiring his new clothes with great interest.

The chamberlains, who were to carry the train of his cloak, did not dare to show that they saw nothing. They bent down with their hands toward the floor just as if they were picking it up and pretended to be holding something in the air.

So the emperor went in procession under the rich canopy, and everyone in the streets said, "Oh, here comes the emperor in his new clothes! How fine he looks!" No one would admit that he could see nothing, for that would have shown that he was not fit for his job, or a fool.

"But he has nothing on!" a little boy cried out suddenly.

"Did you hear what the child said?" asked his father. And people began repeating in whispers what the little boy had said: "But he has nothing on!" And then they began to say it out loud: "But he has nothing on! The emperor has no clothes!"

It seemed to the emperor that they were right, but he thought to himself, I must go on with the procession.

And he held his head up higher than ever, and the chamberlains held on tighter than ever to the cloak which did not exist at all.

But in his heart of hearts the emperor knew that the little boy would make a better emperor than he.

THE SHEPHERDESS AND THE CHIMNEY SWEEP

There was once a little Shepherdess made of china, who lived on a mantelpiece next to a little Chimney sweep made of china.

The Shepherdess was very pretty. Her shoes were painted gold and her dress was covered in red roses. She also had a golden hat and held a shepherd's crook in her dainty hand.

The Chimney sweep was very handsome. He had rosy cheeks and not so much as one smut of soot on the end of his nose, but his jacket and trousers were coal black and he leaned on a ladder.

On the other side of the room there was a huge old cupboard decorated with flowers and leaves and stags with their antlers, all carved out of the very dark wood. And carved on the door of the cupboard was a strange figure with the face of a man, the legs of a goat, a long beard, and horns on

27

his head. There he stood, grinning horribly. The children of the house called him General Sir Billy-goat-bandy-legs, which is quite a mouthful.

General Sir Billy-goat-bandy-legs could not keep his eyes off the pretty little Shepherdess but she was in love with the Chimney sweep and he with her. They hoped to get married one day.

Close by them on the mantelpiece stood a much bigger ornament. This was an old Chinese man with a head that could nod. He too was made of china and he liked to pretend he was the little Shepherdess's grandfather. He was very keen for her to marry General Sir Billy-goat-bandy-legs.

"He will be an excellent husband!" said the old Chinese man. "He has a whole cupboard full of silver, to say nothing of what he keeps hidden in all those drawers!"

"I won't go into that dark cupboard!" said the little Shepherdess.

"Don't be silly!" cried the old Chinese man. "Why, come to think of it, there's no reason why the wedding should not take place tonight!" And with that he nodded his head and fell asleep.

But the little Shepherdess cried and looked at

her sweetheart the china Chimney sweep.

"Oh please, please," she said, "come with me out into the wide world, for we can't stay here."

"I'll do anything to make you happy," replied the little Chimney sweep. "Let us start at once! I think I can earn enough money for both of us by sweeping chimneys."

"If only we were safely down from the mantelpiece," said the little Shepherdess. "I shall not be happy until we are out in the wide world."

And the Chimney sweep comforted her and showed her where to put her little foot on the carved corners of the mantelpiece. He brought his ladder too, to help her, and they were soon together down on the floor. But when they looked up at the old cupboard there was great commotion going on there. All the carved stags were bending their heads, raising their antlers, and craning their necks and General Sir Billy-goat-bandy-legs seemed to be leaping up.

"They're running away! They're running away!" he yelled at the old Chinese man.

The Shepherdess and the Chimney sweep trembled and looked up at the mantelpiece. The old Chinese man had woken up and was rocking backward and forward.

"Oh! He's coming after us!" cried the little Shepherdess, nearly falling over in fright.

"I know!" said the Chimney sweep. "Let's creep into that big bowl over there. We could hide in the lavender and rose petals!"

"That won't be any good," said the Shepherdess. "The old Chinese man and the bowl nearly got married long ago, and I think she might tell him where we are. No, there's nothing left for us but to go out into the wide world."

"Do you really feel brave enough to go into the wide world with me?" asked the Chimney sweep. "Do you realize just how big the world is and that we can never come back here again?"

"I do," she replied.

And the Chimney sweep looked at her tenderly and said: "The way is through the chimney. I know how to find my way through there. If you really have the courage to crawl up it with me we'll climb so high that they can't possibly catch us, and at the very top there's an opening that leads out into the wide world."

And he led her to the fireplace.

"It looks very dark in there," said the Shepherdess, but she still went with him.

"Now we are in the chimney," said the little sweep, "and look, look! Up there a beautiful star is shining."

And it was a real star in the sky, which shone

straight down upon them, as if it wanted to show them the way. Up and up they climbed. It was a long way, and very steep, but the Chimney sweep helped the Shepherdess up. He held her hand and showed her the best places to put her little china feet and at last they reached the top of the chimney and they sat down, for they were desperately tired, as they well might be.

The sky with all its stars was high above, and all the roofs of the town deep below them. They looked all around—far, far out into the world. The poor Shepherdess had never imagined what it would really look like. She leaned her little head on the Chimney sweep's shoulder, and she wept so bitterly that the gold ran down off her sash.

"I can't bear it," she said. "The world is too large! If only I were back on the mantelpiece. I shall never be happy until I am there once again. Now, I followed you out into the wide world, so, if you really love me, you must go back with me."

The Chimney sweep reminded her of the old Chinese man and of General Sir Billy-goat-bandy-legs and their plans for her, but she sobbed bitterly and kissed her little Chimney sweep so that he could not help giving in to her, though it was foolish.

And so with much difficulty they climbed down the chimney again. It was not at all pleasant. And there they stood in the dark fireplace and listened to find out what was going on in the room. It was very quiet, so they looked in and there lay the old Chinese man in the middle of the floor. He had fallen off the mantelpiece trying to chase after

them, and now he had broken into three pieces. His back had come off all in one piece, and his head had rolled into a corner. General Sir Billy-goat-bandy-legs stood where he always stood, grinning and staring.

"How terrible!" said the little Shepherdess. "The old grandfather has fallen to pieces, and it is our fault. I shall never get over it!" and she wrung her little hands.

"He can be mended! He can be mended!" said the Chimney sweep. "Don't get so upset. If they glue his back together and put a good rivet in his neck he will be as good as new and still be able to say an unkind thing to us yet."

"Do you think so?" she cried.

So they climbed back up to the mantelpiece.

"Well here we are again!" sighed the Chimney sweep. "We might as well not have bothered to run away."

"Oh, I do hope the old grandfather can be mended!" said the Shepherdess. "I wonder if it costs a lot of money?"

And sure enough he was mended. The family had his back glued together and fixed a rivet into his neck. He was as good as new, but he could no longer nod.

"You have become very haughty since you fell to pieces," said General Sir Billy-goat-bandy-legs. "I don't think you have any reason to give yourself such airs. Am I to marry her or not?"

And the Chimney sweep and the little Shepherdess looked at the old Chinese man most anxiously, for they were afraid he might nod. But he could not do that anymore, and he did not want to admit that he had a rivet in his neck. So the Shepherdess and the Chimney sweep stayed together and loved one another until the end of their days.

THE STEADFAST TIN SOLDIER

There were once twenty-five tin soldiers who were brothers, because they had all come from one old tin spoon. They shouldered their rifles and looked straight ahead. Their uniforms were red and blue and very splendid. The first words they heard in the world were "Tin soldiers!" A little boy shouted them and clapped his hands when he opened the box of soldiers on his birthday and set them out on the table.

The soldiers all looked exactly the same except for the one which had been made last of all. There had not been enough tin to finish him, but he stood as firmly upon his one leg as the others on their two. It was this soldier who became so special.

There were many other birthday presents on the table, but the best one of all was a castle made of cardboard. Through the little windows you could see straight into the hall. In front of the castle there were some little trees and a tiny mirror for a lake. Toy swans swam on this lake. It all looked very pretty, but even prettier was a little lady standing at the door of the castle. She was cut out of paper and was wearing a muslin dress with blue ribbon over her shoulders that looked like a scarf. In the middle of this ribbon was a shining tinsel rose as big as her whole face. The little lady stretched out both her arms, for she was a dancer, and then she lifted one leg so far behind her that the Tin Soldier could not see it at all, and thought that, like himself, she had only one leg.

Now there's the wife for me, he thought, but she is very grand. She lives in a castle and I have only a box, and there are twenty-five of us in that. It is no place for her. But I must try to make friends with her.

And he hid behind a snuffbox that was on the table and watched the little dainty lady, who went on standing on tiptoe on one leg without losing her balance.

When evening came, all the other tin soldiers were put into their box, and the people in the house went to bed. Now it was the toys' turn to play games. The nutcracker turned somersaults, the pencil scribbled on the table, and the tin soldiers rattled in their box but could not lift the lid. There was so much noise that the canary woke up and began to recite poetry. The only two who did not move from their places were the Tin Soldier and the dancing lady: she balanced on tiptoes on one leg and stretched out both her arms; and he stood there patiently on his one leg and never turned his eyes away from her.

Suddenly the clock struck twelve—and a goblin sprang out of the snuffbox.

"Tin Soldier!" said the Goblin. "Don't you know it's rude to stare?"

But the Tin Soldier pretended not to hear him.

"Just you wait till tomorrow!" said the Goblin.

But in the morning when the children got up, the Tin Soldier was left by the window; and whether it was the Goblin or a draft that did it, the window suddenly flew open, and the soldier fell out. It was a long fall and he landed head first between the paving stones.

The little boy ran down to look for him, but though he almost trod on him he did not see him.

If only the soldier had cried out,
"Here I am!" But he did not think it right to call
out loudly, because he was a soldier.

It began to rain so the little boy went back into
the house. When at last the rain stopped, two poor
boys came by.

"Look!" said one of them. "There's a tin soldier.
Let's fish him out and make him a boat."

And they made a boat out of an old newspaper,
and put the Tin Soldier in it. He sailed down the
gutter and the two boys ran beside him and
clapped their hands. The water was high in that
gutter and running fast because of that heavy rain.
The paper boat rocked up and down, and spun
around and around so giddily that the Tin Soldier
trembled; but he remained steadfast and calm and
looked straight ahead and shouldered his rifle.

All at once the boat shot into a long drain, and
it became as dark as it had been in his box.

Where am I going now? he thought. Is this the
Goblin's doing? Or was it an accident? Oh, if only
the little lady was here with me in the boat I
wouldn't care how dark it was.

Suddenly a great water rat leaped out at him.

"Where's your passport?" said the rat. "Give me your passport."

But the Tin Soldier did not speak and held his rifle tighter than ever.

The boat went on, but the rat came after it. He gnashed his teeth and called out to the whirling bits of straw and wood:

"Stop him! Stop him! He hasn't paid his fare! He hasn't shown his passport!"

The stream was getting stronger and stronger. The Tin Soldier could see bright daylight ahead but he also heard a roaring noise, because where the drain ended the water flowed into a huge canal, and for him that was as dangerous as it is for us to be swept over a waterfall.

But he was already so near it that he could not stop. The boat was swept out. The poor Tin Soldier held himself as stiffly as he could and did not bat an eyelid. The boat whirled around and around. It was so full of water it was bound to sink. The Tin Soldier was up to his neck in water. The boat was sinking; the paper was coming undone and the water closed over the soldier's head.

He thought of the pretty little dancer and how he would never see her again.

The paper fell to bits, but at that very moment the Tin Soldier was snapped up by a great fish.

Oh, how dark it was in the fish's body! It was even darker than in the drain tunnel and narrow too. But the Tin Soldier never moved. He just lay there shouldering his rifle.

The fish swam to and fro and then suddenly became quite still. Then something flashed through the fish like lightning, and a voice said, "Oh, look. There's the Tin Soldier!" The fish had been caught, carried to market, bought, and taken into the kitchen where the cook had cut him open with a large knife. She now took the soldier out and carried him into the next room, where everyone started wondering how he had found his way into a fish. Someone put him on the table, and—what strange things happen in the world! The Tin Soldier was in the very room he had been in before his adventures began. The same children were there and the same toys. And there was the pretty castle with the graceful little dancer! She was still balancing herself on one leg. She was brave and patient too. The Tin Soldier felt like crying tin tears, but soldiers do not weep. He simply looked at her, but they did not speak.

Then suddenly the little boy picked up the Tin Soldier and flung him into the stove. Who knows why? Perhaps it was the doing of the Goblin in the snuffbox.

The Tin Soldier stood there glowing. The heat was terrible, but whether this heat came from the fire or from love he did not know. All his paint had peeled off. He looked at the little lady, she looked at him, and he felt that he was melting; but he still stood steadfast, shouldering his rifle. Then suddenly someone opened the door. The draft of air caught the dancer, and she flew like a butterfly to the Tin Soldier and flashed up in a flame, and was gone. Then the Tin Soldier melted down into a lump, and when the servant emptied the ashes out next day, she found him in the shape of a little tin heart. All that was left of the dancer was the tinsel rose, and that was burned as black as a coal.

THE UGLY DUCKLING

One glorious summer, when the cornfields were yellow, and the stork was striding about on his long legs and chattering in the Egyptian he had learned from his mother, a duck was sitting on her nest waiting for her eggs to hatch. She was tired and lonely. The other ducks were too busy swimming about in the canal to come and cackle with her.

At last the eggshells began to crack. "Peep, peep!" cried the little ducklings, sticking out their heads.

"Cheep, cheep!" they said, and they all came popping out, looking all around them under the green leaves; and the mother let them look as much as they chose, for green is good for the eyes.

"How big the world is!" said the ducklings.

"And that's not all of it!" said their mother.

"It goes right to the other side of the garden, but I have never been there yet. I hope you've all hatched out now," she said and stood up.

"Oh no! You haven't! The biggest egg is still there. I hope it hatches soon; I am so tired." And she sat down again.

At last the huge egg cracked open. "Cheep! Cheep!" said the ducklings and crept out. It was very large and very ugly. The mother duck looked at it.

"What a very large duckling," she said. "None of the others look like that: perhaps it's a turkey chick? We shall soon find out. It will have to go into the water, even if I have to push it in myself."

The next day the mother duck went down to the water with all her little ones. "Quack! Quack!" she said, and one duckling after another plunged in after her. The water closed over their heads, but they came up at once and swam beautifully, and the ugly gray duckling swam with them.

"No, it's not a turkey," said the mother duck. "Look how well it swims and how proudly it holds its head. It is my own child and really quite

pretty, if you look at it properly. Quack! Quack! Come with me children, and I'll show you the big wide world!"

And she took the ducklings to the poultry yard. The other ducks stared at them and said rudely: "Look at them all! As if there were not enough of us already! And just look at the ugly one!" And one duck flew up and bit the Ugly Duckling in the neck.

"Leave it alone," said the mother, "it's not doing any harm."

"Yes, but it's too big and too peculiar," said the duck who had bitten it.

"I know he's not pretty," said the mother duck, "but he swims as well as the others, if not better. He is a drake," she said. "I think he will be very strong."

And she took her family home. But wherever he went, the Ugly Duckling was bitten and pushed around and jeered at by all the ducks and all the chickens.

"He is too big!" they all said.

The poor duckling was very unhappy, and things only grew worse and worse. He was chased by everyone. Even his brothers and sisters were horrid to him and said, "If only the cat would catch you, you ugly creature!" And the mother duck said, "If only you were far away!" And the other ducks bit him, and the chickens pecked him, and the girl who had to feed the poultry kicked him.

In the end he ran off and flew over the fence, and all the little birds in the bushes flew away in fear.

That is because I am so ugly! thought the duckling. And he flew on farther until he came to the great moor, where the wild ducks lived. Tired and miserable he rested through the night.

Toward morning the wild ducks flew up and looked at their new companion.

"What sort of a duck are you?" they asked. "You are very ugly!"

For two days the Ugly Duckling lay in the reeds. Then two wild geese, or, rather, two wild ganders arrived. It was not long since they had hatched themselves and that's why they were so cheeky.

"Listen my friend," said one of them. "You're so ugly that I like you. Why don't you come with us? Near here there are some lovely wild geese, all unmarried. You could marry one of them even though you are so ugly."

Suddenly, there were two loud bangs and the two ganders fell down dead in the swamp, and the

water all around them became bloodred.

"Bang! Bang!" and whole flocks of wild geese rose up from the reeds. A great hunt was going on. The hunters were lying in wait all over the moor, and some were even sitting up in the branches of the trees. Blue smoke rose up like clouds over the dark trees, and the hunting dogs came—splash, splash!—into the swamp, flattening the rushes and the reeds. The Ugly Duckling was terrified and hid his head under his wing; but at that moment a terrifyingly big dog came panting up to the duckling. His tongue was hanging out and his eyes gleamed horribly. He sniffed at the duckling, bared his sharp teeth, and then: splash, splash!—off he went.

"That was lucky!" sighed the duckling. "I am so ugly that even the dog does not want to bite me!"

And he went on hiding while the guns blazed and shots rattled through the reeds. At last silence fell, but the poor duckling waited several hours before he got up and then he hurried away as fast as he could. He ran on over the fields and the meadows until he came to a broken-down hut. The Ugly Duckling slipped through the open door.

An old woman lived in this hut with her cat and her hen. When the cat saw the strange duckling she began to purr, and the hen began to cluck.

"What's all the noise about?" said the woman, looking around, but she could not see very well and so she thought the duckling was a farm duck that had strayed.

"What a piece of luck!" she said. "Now I shall have ducks' eggs. I hope it is not a drake."

The duckling was allowed to stay for three weeks, but no eggs came. And the cat was master of the house, and the hen was the lady and thought the world of herself.

"Can you lay eggs?" she asked.

"No!" said the Ugly Duckling.

"Then kindly hold your tongue."

And the cat said, "Can you curve your back, and purr, and give out sparks?"

"No," said the Ugly Duckling.

"Then you cannot have anything of interest to say," said the cat.

And the duckling sat sadly in a corner.

Then the fresh air and the sunshine streamed in; he suddenly felt such a strange longing to swim that he could not help telling the hen about it.

"What are you talking about?" cried the hen. "You don't do anything all day and that's why you have these funny ideas. Why don't you purr like cat or lay eggs like me?"

"But it is so lovely to swim on the water!" said the duckling. "So refreshing to let it close over one's head and to dive down to the bottom."

"Have you gone crazy?" said the hen. "Ask the cat about it—he's the cleverest animal I know—ask him if he likes to swim on the water or to dive down: I won't speak for myself. Ask our mistress, the old woman: no one in the world is cleverer than she. Do you think she has any desire to swim and to let the water close above her head?"

"You don't understand me," said the duckling. "I think I will go out into the wild world."

"Yes, do go," replied the hen.

And the duckling went away. It swam on the water, and dived, but every creature was unkind to him because he was ugly.

Fall came. The leaves in the forest turned yellow and brown; the wind caught them so that they danced about, and it was very cold. The clouds hung low, heavy with snowflakes, and on the fence

stood a raven, crying, "Croak! Croak!"

The poor little duckling certainly did not have a good time.

One evening, as the sun was setting, there came a whole flock of great handsome birds out of the bushes. They were dazzlingly white, with long curved necks. They were swans. They made a strange harsh cry, spread their glorious great wings, and flew away to warmer lands. They flew so high, so high! And the little Ugly Duckling felt quite strange as he watched them. He swam around and around in circles, stretched out his neck toward them, and uttered such a strange loud cry that he frightened himself.

He could not forget those beautiful, happy birds. He did not know the name of the birds or where they were flying, but he loved them more than he had ever loved anyone. He was not at all envious of them. How could he think of wishing to possess such loveliness as they had? He would just have been glad if they had enjoyed his company—the poor ugly creature!

The winter grew bitterly cold. The duckling was forced to swim about in the water, to stop himself from freezing altogether, but every night the hole he swam about in became smaller and smaller. At last he became so exhausted, that he lay quite still, and so froze in the ice.

Early in the morning a peasant came by, and when he saw what had happened, he took his wooden shoe, broke the ice-crust to pieces, and carried the duckling home. The duckling soon revived in the warmth. The children wanted to play with him, but the duckling thought they would hurt him, and in his terror flew into the milk-pan, so that the milk spilled everywhere. The peasant's wife clapped her hands, at which the duckling flew down into the butter-churn and then into the flour-barrel and out again. He looked such a mess that the woman screamed and hit out at him with the poker. The children fell over each other in their

efforts to catch the duckling; and they laughed and screamed. Luckily the door was open, so the poor creature was able to slip out between the shrubs into the newly fallen snow; and there it lay quite exhausted.

But it would be too sad if I were to tell you about all the suffering the duckling had to go through that winter. He lay out on the moor among the reeds, and when the sun began to shine again and the larks to sing the duckling began to flap his wings. They beat the air more strongly than before and carried him strongly away. Before he knew how it happened he found himself in a great garden where the elder trees smelled sweet and bent their long green branches over the canal that wound through the garden. It was a beautiful spring day, and from the bushes came three glorious white swans. They rustled their wings and swam lightly on the water. The duckling recognized the splendid creatures and felt a strange sadness.

I will fly away to them, to the royal birds, and they will kill me for daring to come anywhere near them. But I don't care. Better to be killed by them than to be chased by ducks, and pecked by fowls, and pushed about by the girl who takes care of the poultry yard, and to suffer hunger in winter!

And he flew out across the water and swam toward the beautiful swans. They looked at him and came sailing toward him with outspread wings.

"Kill me!" cried the Ugly Duckling, and he bent his head down, expecting nothing but death.

But what did he see in the clear water? He saw his own image—he was no longer an ugly dark gray bird, but—a swan! It does not matter where you are born. If you are a swan, you are a swan!

And now the great swans swam around him and stroked him with their beaks. Some children came into the garden and threw bread and corn into the water. The youngest one cried, "There's a new swan!" and the other children shouted joyfully, "Yes, a new one has arrived!" And they clapped their hands and danced about and ran to their father and mother. They all threw bread and cake into the water and said, "The new one is the most beautiful of all! So young and handsome!

Then he felt quite ashamed and hid his head under his wings, for he did not know what to do—he was so happy but not at all proud. He thought how he had been persecuted and despised, and now he heard them saying that he was the most beautiful of all birds. The elder tree was bending its branches over the water, and the sun was shining. Then he rustled his wings, lifted his slender neck, and spoke from the depths of his heart: "I never dreamed of so much happiness when I was still the Ugly Duckling!"

THE LITTLE MERMAID

Far out at sea the water is as blue as the petals of the most beautiful cornflower, and as clear as the purest glass. But it is also very deep. The sea people live down there, and the strangest plants and flowers grow down there. The fish glide among them, just as up here the birds fly in and out of the trees. In the deepest spot of all lies the Sea King's castle: the walls are made of coral and the windows of the clearest amber and the roof is made of shells.

The Sea King had been without a wife for many years, so his old mother kept house for him. She wore twelve oysters on her tail, while other people were only allowed to wear six. She was very fond of her six granddaughters, the little Sea Princesses. They were all pretty, but the youngest was the prettiest of them all. Her skin was as soft as a rose petal, her eyes were as blue as the deepest sea, but, like all the rest, she had no feet, for her body ended in a fishtail.

All day long the princesses played in the castle and the fish swam straight up to them, ate out of their hands, and let themselves be stroked.

Outside the castle, in the garden, the fruit glowed like gold and the flowers like flames of fire. The earth itself was fine sand and a strange blue light lay upon everything as if one were high up in the sky, rather than at the bottom of the sea. When it was calm the sun appeared like a purple flower streaming with light.

Each of the little princesses had her own flowerbed where she could grow whatever she liked. One flowerbed was in the shape of a whale; another like a little seahorse, but the youngest

56

princess made hers quite round, like the sun, and grew flowers in it which gleamed red as the sun itself. She was a strange child, quiet and thoughtful, and when the other sisters set out all the beautiful things they had been given from ships that had sunk, she never asked for anything except a pretty marble statue of a boy, carved out of white stone.

There was nothing she liked more than to hear about the world of men. The old grandmother had to tell her everything she knew about ships and towns, and men and animals. It seemed wonderful to her that up on the earth the flowers had a scent, for they had none down at the bottom of the sea, and that the trees were green, and that the fish which one saw there among the trees could sing. What the grandmother called fish were birds, but the princess could not understand them in any other way, for she had never seen a bird.

"When you are fifteen," said the grandmother, "you will be allowed to rise up out of the sea, and sit on the rocks in the moonlight, and watch the great ships sailing by. Then you will see forests and towns!"

The youngest princess still had five more years to wait before she could come up from the bottom of the sea and look at our world. But each princess in turn promised to tell the others what she had seen and what she had thought the most beautiful on the first day of her visit.

Many a night the youngest princess looked up through the dark blue water where she could see the moon and stars shining. When something like a black cloud passed among them, she knew that it was either a whale swimming over her head or a ship full of people; little did they know that a pretty little mermaid was standing down below, stretching up her arms toward the keel of their ship.

When the eldest princess was fifteen years old, she was allowed to swim up and look at our world.

When she came back, she had a hundred things to tell, but the finest thing, she said, was lying in the moonlight on a sandbank in the quiet sea and looking at the coast where lights twinkled like a hundred stars, and listening to the sound of church bells.

Oh, how the youngest sister dreamed of the great city with its bright lights and noise, and thought she could hear the church bells ringing, even down in the depths where she was.

The following year the second sister was allowed to go up through the water and swim wherever she pleased. She rose up just as the sun was setting, which she said was the most beautiful sight. The whole sky turned to gold, she said, and the clouds floated over her head, while beneath them flew a line of wild swans, like a long white veil.

When the next sister went up, who was the boldest of them all, she swam up a broad river and saw green hills covered in vines and heard how the birds sing. The sun was so warm that she often had to dive under the water to cool her face. In a little

bay she found some small humans splashing about in the water. She wanted to play with them, but they ran away from her and a little black animal came. It was a dog, but she had never seen a dog. It barked and frightened her so she swam down to the sea again.

The fourth sister was not so brave. She stayed out in the middle of the wild sea. She saw ships, but only in the far distance, and dolphins turning somersaults, and great whales spouting water from their nostrils, so that it looked like hundreds of fountains.

The fifth sister's birthday came in the winter, and so she saw what the others had not seen. The sea was emerald green, and huge icebergs floated past. They came in all shapes and shone like diamonds. She sat on one of them and let the wind play with her long hair.

Toward the evening the sky clouded over. There was thunder and lightning and black waves crashed against the icebergs. The sails were lowered on all the ships and she heard sailors crying out in fear. But she sat quietly on her floating iceberg and watched the forked lightning flash across the sea.

The five sisters were grown up now and were allowed to swim up above the water whenever they liked. Often in the evenings they took each other by the hand and rose up in a row over the water. They had lovely voices, more beautiful than

any human could have, and when a storm was coming, and they could see that ships would sink, they swam around the ships and sang lovely songs, which told how beautiful it was at the bottom of the sea, and begged the sailors not to be afraid to come down below. But the sailors did not understand the words and thought it was the storm sighing.

When the sisters rose up hand in hand through the water the youngest sister stood all alone gazing after them. She felt like crying, but mermaids cannot cry and for this reason suffer far more than those who can.

"Oh, I can't wait to be fifteen!" she said. "I know I shall love the world up there very much, and the people who live there."

At last her fifteenth birthday arrived.

"Now you are grown up," said the grandmother, "come, let me dress you up like your sisters."

And she put a wreath of white lilies in the Little Mermaid's hair and ordered eight great oysters to clip themselves to the princess's tail.

"But that hurts!" said the Little Mermaid.

"Yes," replied her grandmother, "a princess must suffer pain."

The sun had just set when the youngest princess lifted her head above the sea, but all the clouds were still rosy and golden and in the pale green sky the evening stars shimmered brightly. The air was warm and the sea quite calm. A great ship with three masts lay at anchor, lit up by hundreds of colored lanterns. The Little Mermaid could hear the sound of music and singing and so she swam straight to the cabin window, and looked in. She saw many people standing inside dressed in their best clothes. But the handsomest of all was the young prince with the big dark eyes: he was certainly not much more than sixteen years old. It was his birthday, and that was the reason for all this feasting. The sailors were dancing on the deck, and when the young prince came out, more than a hundred rockets rose into the air. They shone like day which startled the Little Mermaid, who dived under the water, but she soon put out her head again and then it seemed as if all the stars in the sky

were falling down on her.

She had never seen fireworks. Great suns spurted fire, glorious fiery fishes flew up into the blue air, and everything was mirrored in the clear blue sea. The ship was so brightly lit up that she could see everything. How handsome the young prince was! He shook hands with everyone and smiled, while the music rang out in the warm night.

It grew late, but the Little Mermaid could not take her eyes off the ship and the beautiful prince. The party came to an end but now the waves rose higher, great clouds came up, and in the distance there was lightning. A storm was blowing up so the sailors put up the sails. The ship flew across the wild sea. The waters rose up like great black mountains, but like a swan the ship dived into the valleys between these high waves, and then let itself be lifted on high again. To the Little Mermaid this seemed like a game, but to the sailors it looked very different. The ship groaned and creaked, the mainmast snapped in two like a thin reed and the ship keeled over while the water rushed into the hold. Now the Little Mermaid understood that the people were in great danger.

By a flash of lightning she could see everyone on board. She tried desperately to find the prince, and when the ship broke up she saw him sink into the sea. She was very glad, for now he would come down to her. But then she remembered that people cannot live under the water, and that when he got down to her father's palace he would certainly be dead. No, he must not die. Diving down deep under the water, then rising again above the waves, she at last found the prince, who could hardly swim another stroke in that stormy sea. He would have died if the Little Mermaid had not come. She held his head up over the water and then allowed the waves to carry them wherever they wanted.

When morning came the storm was over. Of the ship nothing was to be seen. The sun came up but the prince's eyes remained closed. The mermaid kissed his forehead and stroked his wet hair. He reminded her of the marble statue in her little garden: she kissed him again and hoped that he would live.

They came to dry land. The mermaid saw high mountains, green forests, and a building which she did not know was a convent. The sea formed a little bay there, so in she swam and laid the prince on the sand.

Suddenly bells rang in the big white building, and many young girls came walking through the garden. The Little Mermaid hid behind some rocks that stood up out of the water, splashed some sea foam on her hair and neck, so that no one could see her, and waited to see who would find the poor prince.

Before long a young girl discovered him. She seemed startled, but only for a moment. She fetched more people and the mermaid saw that the prince had come back to life and that he was smiling at everyone. But he did not smile at her; for he did not know that she had saved him. The Little Mermaid felt very sad, and when the prince was carried away into the big building she dived sorrowfully under the water and returned to her father's palace.

She had always been gentle and dreamy, but now she became much more so. Her sisters asked her what she had seen when she rose up to the surface, but she would not tell them.

Many an evening and many a morning she went

up to the place where she had left the prince. She saw the fruits of the garden ripen, she saw the snow melt on the high mountain, but she did not see the prince, and so she always returned home sadder than ever. Her only comfort was to sit in her little garden, with her arm around the beautiful marble statue that looked like the prince; but she did not look after her flowers.

At last she could bear it no longer and told the whole story to her sisters, who told the secret to the Little Mermaid's closest friend. She knew who the [rince was—she too had seen the festival on board the ship and she knew where his kingdom was.

"Come, little sister!" said the other princesses, and linking their arms together they rose up out of the sea in a long row in front of the prince's palace.

This palace was built of bright yellow stone, with many marble staircases leading straight down to the sea. Through the clear glass of the windows one could see costly silk hangings and rugs, and walls covered with splendid pictures, and in the middle a great fountain played.

Now that the Little Mermaid knew where the prince lived, she spent many nights there on the water. She swam far closer to the land than any of the others would have dared; indeed she went right under the marble balcony, which threw a broad shadow on the water. Here she sat and watched the young prince, who thought himself quite alone in the bright moonlight.

Many an evening she saw him sailing to the sound of music in his fine boat with the waving flags. She peeped up through the green reeds, and when the wind caught her silver-white veil anyone who saw it thought it was a white swan spreading its wings.

Many a night when the fishermen were on the sea with their torches, she heard them talking about the prince. They said such good things about him that she became even happier that she had saved his life.

She began to love humans and wished she could wander through their world which seemed far larger than her own. For they could speed across the sea in ships, and climb the high hills far above the clouds, and the lands they possessed stretched out in woods and fields farther than her eyes could reach. There was much she wished to know, so she went to the old grandmother, who knew the

upper world, which she called "the countries above the sea," very well.

"If people are not drowned," asked the Little Mermaid, "can they live forever? Do they not die as we die down here in the sea?"

"Yes," replied the old lady. "They too must die and their life is even shorter than ours. We can live to be three hundred years old, but then we are turned into foam on the surface of the water. We do not have an immortal soul. But humans have a soul which lives on after the body has become dust. It goes up to all the shining stars! As we rise up out of the waters and see all the lands of the earth, so they rise up to unknown, glorious places which we never see."

"Why did we not receive an immortal soul?" asked the Little Mermaid sorrowfully. "I would gladly give all the hundreds of years I have to live to be a human being only for one day."

"You must not think that," replied her grand-mother. "We think we are far happier than human beings."

"Then am I to die and turn into foam and never hear the music of the waves, or see the pretty flowers and the red sun? Can I not do anything to win an immortal soul?"

"No!" answered the grandmother. "Only if a man were to love you more than anyone else and marry you, only then could you receive a share of human happiness. He would give a soul to you and yet keep his own. But that can never happen. What we think is beautiful here in the sea—the fishtail—they think is ugly on the earth: they don't understand it. There one must have two clumsy supports, which they call legs, to be beautiful."

Then the Little Mermaid sighed, and looked sadly at her fishtail.

"Let us be glad!" said the grandmother. "Let us enjoy the three hundred years we have to live. This evening we shall have a ball."

It was a splendid sight, such as is never seen on earth, and all night long the sea people danced to their own lovely songs in voices more beautiful than anything heard on earth. The Little Mermaid sang the most sweetly of all, and for a moment she felt happy, for she knew she had the loveliest voice of all in the sea or on the earth. But soon she thought again of the world above her; she could not forget the prince or her sorrow at not having an immortal soul like his. So she crept out of the palace and went and sat sadly in her little garden.

Then she heard sailors' pipes sounding through the waters, and thought, now he is certainly sailing above me, my beloved prince in whose hand I should like to lay my life's happiness. I will dare everything to win him and a soul. While my sisters are still dancing I will go to the Sea Witch. I have always been terrified of her, but perhaps she can help me.

So the Little Mermaid set out for the foaming whirlpools behind which the Witch lived. She had never been that way before. No flowers grew there, no sea grass; only the naked gray sand stretched out toward the whirlpools, where the water rushed round like roaring mill wheels sucking everything into the deep.

Behind the whirlpool lay the Witch's house in the middle of a strange forest, where all the trees looked like hundred-headed snakes growing up out of the earth. All the branches were long slimy arms, with fingers like wriggling worms; they clung to everything they got hold of and never let it go. The Little Mermaid's heart beat with fear, and she was about to turn back, but then she thought of the prince and the human soul, and her courage came back again. She tied her long hair tightly around her head, so that the snakelike trees could not get hold of her. She put her arms by her sides and shot forward as a fish shoots through the water, among the ugly trees which stretched out their slimy arms and fingers after her. She saw that each of them was holding something in its hundreds of little arms. Skulls and skeletons of people who had perished at sea, ships' oars, and the bones of land animals stared out at her. The Little Mermaid was terrified.

But she bravely went on until she came to the Witch's house in the middle of this forest. There sat the Sea Witch feeding a toad just as we might feed a canary with sugar, while water snakes crawled all over her.

"I know what you want, my foolish, pretty princess," said the Sea Witch. "You want to get rid of your fishtail and have two legs instead like the people of the earth, so that the young prince will fall in love with you, and you may get an immortal soul." And the Witch cackled so loudly that the toad and the water snakes fell to the ground.

"Very well, then! I will prepare a magic potion for you, with which you must swim to land tomorrow before the sun rises and sit down there and drink it. Then your tail will shrivel up and become what the people of the earth call legs, but it will hurt you. Everyone who sees you will say you are the prettiest human being they ever saw. You will keep your graceful walk—no dancer will be able to move as lightly as you—but every step you take will feel as if you are treading on sharp knives. If you can bear all this, I can help you."

"Yes," said the Little Mermaid. She was trembling, but she kept thinking of the prince and the immortal soul.

"But, remember," said the Witch, "when you have once received a human form, you can never be a mermaid again. You can never go back to your sisters or to your father's palace; and if you do not win the prince's love, and if he does not marry you, you will not receive a soul. On the first morning after he has married another princess, your heart will break and you will turn into foam on the water."

"I will do it," said the Little Mermaid, turning as pale as death.

"But you must pay me, too," said the Witch, "and I ask a hard payment. You have the finest voice of all down here, and with it you hope to win the prince, but you must give your voice to me. It is the best thing you possess, and I must have it for my potion. I must put my own blood into it too, so that the potion will be as sharp as a two-edged sword."

"But if you take away my voice," said the Little Mermaid, "what will be left to me?"

"Your beautiful shape," replied the Witch, "your graceful walk, and your speaking eyes:  because of those the prince will fall in love with you. Now! Put out your little tongue, and I will cut it off for my payment, and then you shall have the strong potion."

"It shall be so," said the Little Mermaid.

And the Witch fetched her cauldron. First she cleaned the cauldron out with the snakes, which she tied up in a big knot; then she scratched herself, and let her black blood drop into it. Steam rose up in the strangest forms, enough to frighten anyone. The Witch kept throwing horrible things into the cauldron and when it had boiled thoroughly, there was a sound like the weeping of a crocodile. At last the potion was ready. It looked like the purest water.

The Witch gave it to the Little Mermaid. Then she cut off the Little Mermaid's tongue, so that she could neither sing nor speak.

She could see her father's palace. The ball was long since over and everyone was asleep, but she did not dare go back now that she was dumb and was about to leave them forever. She felt as if her heart would break. She blew a thousand kisses toward the palace, and then she rose up through the dark blue sea.

The sun had not yet risen when she came to the prince's castle and climbed the marble staircase. By the light of the moon the Little Mermaid drank the sharp, burning potion and it seemed as if a two-edged sword went through her delicate body. She fainted away and lay as if she were dead. When the sun shone out over the sea she woke up in pain, but there standing before her was the handsome young prince. He stared at her with his dark eyes, so that she looked away shyly, and then she saw that her fishtail had gone, and that she had the prettiest pair of feet a little girl could have. But she had no clothes, so she covered herself with her long hair.

The Prince asked where she had come from, and she just looked at him sadly with her blue eyes, for she could not speak. Then he took her by the hand and led her into the castle. Each step she took was, just as the Witch had said, as if she had been treading on sharp knives, but she bore it joyfully. At the Prince's right hand she moved on, light as a soap bubble, and he, like everyone else, was astonished at her graceful swaying movements.

She was given fine clothes, and although she was certainly the most beautiful creature in the castle, she could neither sing nor speak. Lovely girls dressed in silk and gold came forward and sang to the prince and his guests. One girl sang better than all the others and the Prince smiled at her and clapped his hands. Then the Little Mermaid felt sad because she knew that she had once been able to sing far more sweetly.

Oh! she sighed to herself. If only he knew that I have given away my voice forever to be with him. Then she raised her beautiful slender arms, stood on the tips of her toes, and danced as no one had yet danced. Everyone was struck by her beauty and by her eyes, which spoke directly to the heart.

The prince called her his little foundling and said she must stay with him always. He took her riding with him and walking in the high mountains, and even when everyone could see how her delicate feet bled she just laughed and went on walking.

But at night when everyone was asleep, she went down the broad marble steps and bathed her bleeding feet in the cold sea water, and then she thought of her dear family at the bottom of the sea.

Once at night, her sisters came to see her. They sang sadly as they floated on the water. She beckoned to them, and they recognized her and told her how much they missed her. After that they came every night, and once, in the distance, she saw her old grandmother and her father, with his crown on his head. They stretched out their hands toward her but did not come near her.

Day by day the prince grew to love the Little Mermaid, but he loved her as one loves a dear little child. He never thought of marrying her.

"Do you not love me best of all?" the eyes of the Little Mermaid seemed to say, whenever he kissed her.

"Yes, you are the dearest to me," said the prince, "for you have the best heart of them all! You remind me of a young girl I once saw, but whom I certainly shall not find again. I was shipwrecked and the waves threw me ashore near a convent which some young girls were just leaving. The youngest of them found me and saved my life. I only saw her twice. She was the only one in the world I could marry but you are so like her.

Ah! He does not know that I saved his life,

thought the Little Mermaid. I carried him over the sea to where that convent stands. I hid under the foam and waited to see if anyone would come. I saw the beautiful girl whom he loves better than me. And she sighed deeply for she could not weep.

But if she belongs to that convent, she thought, they will never meet again. But I see him every day. I will take care of him and love him and give up my life for him.

One day the prince's father told him that it was time he found a wife. A fine new ship was prepared to take him to visit the beautiful princess in the neighboring kingdom. The Little Mermaid was not worried: she knew the prince's thoughts far better than anyone else.

"I must obey my father," he said to her. "I must go and see this princess, but no one can make me marry her. If I have to marry, I would choose you, my dear dumb foundling with the speaking eyes, because you remind me of the girl at the convent who saved my life."

And he kissed her so tenderly that she dreamed of happiness and of an immortal soul.

"Aren't you afraid of the sea, my silent child?" said the prince when they stood on the deck of the magnificent ship carrying them to the land of the neighboring king. He told the Little Mermaid about storms and strange fish and what divers had seen at the bottom of the sea. And the Little Mermaid smiled to herself, for she knew far better than he did what it was like down there.

When the ship sailed into the harbor of the neighboring king's splendid city, bells rang and trumpets sounded. Each day there were festivities and dancing every night and at last the princess arrived.

When the Prince saw her he fell to his knees and cried out: "But you are the girl who saved me when I lay on the shore as good as dead! I would know those kind blue eyes anywhere!" And he stood up and kissed the princess.

"Oh, my Little Mermaid," he said. "I am so happy! And I know you are happy too because you love me most of all!"

The Little Mermaid kissed his hand even though her heart was broken, for his wedding morning would bring death to her, and change her into foam on the sea.

Next day all the church bells rang out and the prince and princess were married. The Little Mermaid was dressed in gold and held the bride's train, but she heard nothing of the festive music. She could only think of her death.

That evening the bride and bridegroom went on board the ship. The cannon roared, flags fluttered in the breeze, and in the middle of the ship a golden tent had been set up, where the couple were to sleep in the cool, still night.

The ship set sail. Colored lamps were lit and all the company danced on deck. The Little Mermaid could not help thinking of the first time she had seen such a scene and she joined the dancers. Everyone applauded her, for she danced so beautifully. She did not feel the knifelike pain in her feet because the pain in her heart was so much worse. She knew this was the last evening that she would see the prince for whom she had left her family and home, and sacrificed her beautiful voice, and suffered unheard-of pain every day, about which he had not the slightest idea. It was the last evening she would breathe the same air and see the starry sky and the deep sea. Everlasting night was waiting for her, for she had no soul, and now could not have one. The merriment went on till past midnight, and she laughed and danced with thoughts of death in her heart. The prince kissed his beautiful bride, and hand in hand, they went in to the splendid tent.

It grew quiet on the ship and the Little Mermaid leaned her arms on the rail and gazed out toward the east. The sun's first ray, she knew, would kill her. Then she saw her sisters rising out of the sea. They were pale, and their long hair no longer waved in the wind for it had been cut off.

"We have given it to the Witch," they called, "so that you do not die tonight. She has given us a knife. Look how sharp it is! Before the sun rises you must thrust it into the prince's heart and when warm blood falls on your feet they will grow together again into a fishtail, and you will become a mermaid again and come back to us and live your three hundred years before you become sea foam. Hurry! Hurry! He or you must die before the sun rises! Kill the prince and come back! In a few minutes the sun will rise and you will die!" And they vanished beneath the waves.

The Little Mermaid drew back the curtain from the tent and saw the beautiful bride lying with her head on the prince's shoulder. She bent down and kissed him. Then she looked at the sharp knife and again at the prince. The knife trembled in the mermaid's hands. Then she flung it far away into the waves. One last time she looked with half-closed eyes at the prince; then she threw herself into the sea and turned into white foam.

Now the sun rose up out of the sea, and the Little Mermaid saw hundreds of lovely bright beings floating above her, but no human eye could hear their song and no human eye could see them. They floated through the air without wings, and the Little Mermaid saw that she had a body like theirs and was rising up and up out of the foam.

"Where am I going?" she asked, and her voice sounded like that of those other beings, quite unlike any earthly music.

"To the daughters of the air!" replied the others. "A mermaid can only be given a soul by a human who loves her and marries her. We daughters of the air also have no soul, but we can make ourselves one if we do good deeds for three hundred years. You, poor Little Mermaid, have already done many good deeds and suffered much. By your good works you have risen to the world of spirits and in three hundred years you will be given a soul."

For the first time the Little Mermaid's eyes filled

with tears. She could see the prince and his bride looking sadly at the pearly foam, as if they knew that she had thrown herself into the waves. Unseen, she kissed them both and rose through the golden clouds with the other daughters of the air.

"In three hundred years," she whispered joyfully, "I shall have a soul and find my prince again in paradise."

WHAT THE OLD MAN DOES IS ALWAYS RIGHT

I'd like to tell you a story which was told to me when I was a little boy. Every time I think of this story it seems better than it was before, for it is the same of many people—they get better as they grow older!

You've been out in the country, I'm sure, and seen a really old cottage with a thatched roof, and a stork's nest on the gable—for we can't do without the stork. The walls of the cottage slope outward and the windows are difficult to open. The baking oven bulges out of the wall like a little tubby person. An elder tree hangs over the fence and beneath its branches is a pond on which a few ducks are swimming. There is a dog in the yard, too, who barks at all comers. You know the kind of place.

Well, once there was just such a cottage out in

83

the country, and in it lived an old couple—a peasant and his wife. Their farm was very small but there was one thing that they couldn't do without—and that was a horse who lived on the grass which grew by the side of the road. The old peasant rode into the town on this horse, and often his neighbors borrowed it in return for helping the old couple, round the little farm. But the day came when they decided it would better to sell the horse or exchange it for something that might be more useful to them. But what might this something be?

"You'll know that best, old man," said the wife. "Go to the fair and get rid of the horse for money or make a good exchange; whichever you do will feel right to me. Off you go to the fair!" And she brushed his hat for him and gave him a kiss. So he rode away upon the horse that was to be sold or to be exchanged for something else. Oh yes, the man knew what he was doing all right!

It was very hot and not a cloud to be seen in the sky. The road was very dusty, for many people who were going to the fair were driving, or riding, or walking along it. There was no shelter anywhere from the sun.

The old man saw a farmer trudging along, driving a cow to the fair. The cow was as beautiful as any cow can be.

"I bet she gives good milk," said the old man. "That would be a very good exchange—the cow for the horse."

"Hello, you there with the cow!" he said, "I tell you what—I imagine a horse costs more than a cow, but I don't care about that, a cow would be more useful to me. If you like, we could make an exchange."

"Certainly," said the man, and they exchanged animals.

So that was settled, and the old man could have turned back there and then, for he had done the business he came to do, but since he had made up his mind to go to the fair, he decided to go on just to have a look and so he went on to the town with his cow.

He soon overtook a man who was driving a sheep. It was a good fat sheep, with a fine fleece on its back.

I should like to have that sheep, said our old man to himself, he would find plenty of grass by our fence and in winter we could keep him indoors with us. Perhaps it would be better to have a sheep instead of a cow.

The man with the sheep was quite ready to exchange his sheep for the cow, and the bargain was soon struck. So our old man went along the road with his sheep.

Soon he overtook another man, coming out of a field, carrying a great goose under his arm.

"That's a heavy thing you have there," said our old man. "It has plenty of feathers and plenty of fat, and would look very fine paddling about on our pond. That would be something for my wife—she could make some money out of a goose. She has often said, 'If only we had a goose!'"

So he said to the man: "I'll give you my sheep for your goose, and thank you into the bargain."

The man did not mind in the least and so our old man became the owner of the goose.

By this time he was very near the town. The crowd on the high road grew bigger and bigger. There was a huge crush of men and animals all over the road, even spilling into the tollgate man's potato patch, where his own chicken was strutting about with a string tied to its leg, in case it took fright at the crowd and ran away and got lost. This chicken had short tail feathers and blinked a lot and looked very cunning.

As soon as our old man saw it, he thought, that's the finest chicken I've ever seen in my life! I should like to have that chicken. A chicken can always find a grain or two to eat and can almost keep itself.

"Will you exchange your chicken for my goose?" he asked the tollgate man, who looked at the fat goose and said, "That's not such a bad idea." So they exchanged birds and the old man went off with the chicken.

He had done a good deal of business on his way to the fair, and now he was hot and tired. He wanted something to eat and drink so he went to the inn. He was just about to step in when out came the man who looked after the horses, carrying a sack.

"What's in that sack?" asked the old man.

"Rotten apples," said the man who looked after the horses. "A whole sack full of them, enough to feed the pigs with."

"What a terrible waste!" said the old man. "I should like to take them home to my wife. Last year our old tree only bore a single apple, and we kept it in the cupboard till it went rotten. How pleased she'd be if she had a whole sackful."

"What will you give me in return?" asked the man who looked after the horses.

"What will I give? Why, I'll give my chicken in exchange."

So he handed over the chicken and took the apples, which he carried into the inn. He leaned the sack carefully next to the stove, and then went to the table. But the stove was hot: he had not thought of that. There were many people at the inn, including two Englishmen. These two Englishmen were so rich that their pockets were positively bulging with gold coins.

Suddenly there was a long hissing sound by the stove. It was the apples. They were beginning to cook!

"What is that noise?" said someone.

"I'll tell you all about it," said our old man. And he told the whole story of the horse that he had exchanged for a cow, and all the rest of it, down to the apples.

"Well, your wife will certainly give it to you when you get home!" said one of the two Englishmen. "There will be a rumpus!"

"What? Give me what?" said the old peasant. "She will kiss me, and say, 'What the old man does is always right.'"

"Shall we bet on that?" said the Englishman. "A hundred gold coins to the ton."

"I can only set the apples against that," said our old man, "with myself and my wife thrown in for good measure . . ."

"Done," said the Englishman.

And the bet was made. The landlord's carriage was brought out. The Englishmen got in, the peasant got in and away they went, and soon they arrived at the old man's farm.

"Good evening, dear wife."

"Good evening, dear husband."

"I've made the exchange."

"Of course you have," said the old woman, "you always know what you're doing."

And she kissed him and paid no attention to the strangers, nor did she notice the sack.

"I got a cow in exchange for the horse," said the old man.

"Wonderful!" said the old woman. "What glorious milk we shall now have, and butter and cheese on the table! That was an excellent exchange!"

"Yes, but then I changed the cow for a sheep," said the old man.

"Better still!" cried the wife. "You always think of everything: we have just enough grass for a sheep. Ewe's milk and cheese, and woolen jackets and stockings! You think of everything!"

"But then I changed the sheep for a goose," said the old man.

"Then this year we shall really have roast goose for our Christmas dinner. You are such a dear. You are always thinking of something to give me pleasure."

"But then I gave away the goose for a chicken," said the old man.

"A chicken? That was a good exchange!" replied the old woman. "The chicken will lay eggs and hatch them and before we know where we are, we shall have a whole poultry yard! Oh, that's just what I was wishing for."

"Yes, but I exchanged the chicken for a sack of rotten apples."

"What! I must kiss you for that," cried the wife. "My dear, good husband! Now I'll tell you something. You had hardly left me this morning before I began thinking how I could give you a really  delicious supper this evening. I decided on pancakes with savory herbs. I had eggs, but I wanted herbs. So I went over to the school-mistress's—they have herbs there, I know. I asked her for a handful of herbs. 'Herbs?' she laughed. 'I'm sorry but nothing at all grows in our garden, not even a rotten apple. I couldn't even give you a rotten apple, my dear.' But now I can give her ten, or a whole sackful, and that makes me very happy!" And with that she gave him a noisy kiss.

"Well, I never!" exclaimed both the Englishmen together. "Things going from bad to worse but always cheerful. That's worth every penny of our bet!"

So they paid up their gold to the old man who got a kiss instead of a beating.

Well, that is my story. I heard it when I was a child; and now you have heard it, you too know that "What the old man does is always right."

THE FIR TREE

Out in the forest stood a pretty little Fir Tree. It grew in a good place where there was plenty of sunlight and air. It was surrounded by many larger trees—pines as well as firs, but the little Fir Tree longed to grow bigger. It took no notice of the warm sun and the fresh air, or of the children who came chattering into the forest to look for strawberries and raspberries. Often they passed by with a basketful and would sit down by the little Fir Tree and say, "How pretty that small one is!" But that was not at all what the tree wanted to hear.

During the next year it had grown a new shoot, and the following year it grew even taller. One can always tell by the number of rings it has how many years a tree has been growing.

"Oh, if only I were as big as the others!" sighed

the little Fir, "then I would spread my branches far around, and look out onto the wide world from my top. The birds would build nests in my branches, and when the wind blew I would nod just as proudly as the other trees."

In the winter, when the snow lay all around, white and sparkling, a hare came jumping along, and leaped right over the little Fir Tree, which made him very angry. But when three winters had gone by the little tree had grown so tall that the hare had to run around it.

Oh, to grow and to grow and be old! Surely that's the best thing in the world, thought the tree.

In the fall woodcutters always came and chopped down some of the largest trees and the little Fir Tree shuddered with fear, for the great trees fell to the ground with a crash, and their branches were cut off, so that the trees looked quite bare. Then they were laid on wagons and dragged away. Where were they going? the little Fir Tree wondered.

In the spring, when the swallows and the stork

came, the tree asked them, "Do you know where the trees go? Have you seen them?"

The swallows said "No," but the stork said: "Yes, I think so. I saw many new ships when I flew out of Egypt. They had very tall masts; I think that these were the trees. They smelled like fir. All I can say is that they were tall and stately—very stately."

"I wish I was big enough to go over the sea!" sighed the little Fir Tree. "What kind of thing is this sea, and what does it look like?"

"It would take too long to explain all that," said the stork, and he went away.

"Be happy that you are still young and strong," said the sunbeams.

And the wind and the rain kissed the tree, but the Fir Tree did not care.

At Christmastime quite young trees were cut down; trees which were younger and smaller than this impatient Fir Tree. These beautiful young trees did not have their branches chopped off when they were put on wagons and taken out of the wood.

"Where are they all going?" asked the Fir Tree. "Some are much smaller than me. Why do they keep all their branches? Where are they being taken?"

"We know! We know!" chirped the sparrows. "In the town we are always peeping through the windows, so we know where they go. They get decorated in the most wonderful way you could possibly imagine. We have looked in at the windows and seen them planted in tubs in the warm sitting room, and covered with the most beautiful things—gilt apples, honey-cakes, toys, and hundreds of candles."

"And then?" asked the Fir Tree, trembling through all its branches. "And then? What happens then?"

"Well," said the sparrows, "that's all we saw, but it was wonderful."

"Perhaps that will happen to me one day!" cried the Fir Tree. "That would be even better than traveling across the sea. If only it were Christmas now! Oh, if only I were being carted off! If only I were in the warm sitting room decorated with lovely things. And then? What would happen? It must be something even more wonderful. Why would they decorate me? Oh, I wish this would happen to me!"

"Be happy here with us," said the air and the sunshine. "Be happy here in the woodland."

But the Fir Tree was not at all happy. It grew
and grew and stood there, green, dark green.
The people who saw it said, "That's a
handsome tree!" and at Christmastime it was
cut down before any of the others. The ax cut
deep into its trunk, and the tree fell to the
ground with a sigh: it felt pain and was now
sad at parting from its home. It knew that
it would never again see its dear friends,
the little bushes and flowers—perhaps
not even the birds.

The tree only came to itself when it
was unloaded in a yard with the other
trees and heard a man say, "This one
is the best. We only want this one!"

Now two servants came in
bright uniforms and carried the
Fir Tree into a large beautiful room.
All around the walls hung pictures,
and by the great stove stood huge
Chinese vases with lions on
them.

There were rocking chairs, silken sofas, tables covered with picture books, and hundreds of toys everywhere.

The Fir Tree was put into a great tub filled with sand. The tree trembled! What would happen next? The servants and the children decorated it. On the branches they hung little bags cut out of colored paper. Each bag was filled with candy; golden apples and walnuts hung down as if they grew there, and hundreds of little candles were fastened to the boughs. Dolls that looked exactly like real people hung from other branches, and right at the very top of the tree was fixed a tinsel star. It was magnificent, quite magnificent.

"This evening," said everybody, "this evening the star will shine."

Oh, thought the Fir Tree, if only it were evening already! Oh, I do hope the candles will soon be lit. I wonder if the trees will come out of the forest to look at me?

And the sparrows peep in at the windows? Will I stay here decorated forever and ever?

All these questions gave the tree a backache, and a backache is just as bad for a tree as a headache is for a person.

At last the candles were lighted. What brilliance, what splendor! The Fir Tree trembled so much that one of the candles set fire to a green twig, but the fire was quickly put out.

And now the doors were opened wide and the children rushed in. They stared at the tree silently but only for a minute. Then they started shouting joyfully and dancing around the tree, pulling at their presents.

What are they doing? thought the Fir Tree. What's going on?

The candles burned down, the children pulled the candy off the tree and danced about with their new toys. No one looked at the tree anymore except one old man, who came up and peeped among the branches to see if all the nuts and apples had been eaten.

"A story! A story!" shouted the children and they drew a jolly man toward the tree; and he sat down just beneath it.

"Let's pretend we're in the green wood," he said, "and that the tree can hear my story."

And the jolly man told the story of Klumpey-Dumpey, who was always falling down the stairs and yet in the end married a princess. The Fir Tree stood quite silent and thoughtful; never had the birds in the wood told such a story as that. Klumpey-Dumpey always falling down stairs and yet married a princess!

"Well! Well!" said the Fir Tree. "Who knows? Perhaps I shall fall down the stairs too and marry a princess!" And it looked forward to being decorated again the next evening with candles and toys and fruit.

But in the morning the servants came and dragged him out of the room, and upstairs to the attic, and put him in a dark corner where no daylight shone.

What's the meaning of this? thought the tree. What am I doing here? What's happening?

And he leaned against the wall, and thought, and thought. And he had time enough, for days and nights went by, and nobody came up. The tree seemed to be quite forgotten.

Now it's winter outside, thought the Fir Tree. The earth is hard and covered with snow, and people cannot plant me. I suppose I'm to be sheltered here until spring comes. How thoughtful! How good people are! If only it were not so dark here, and so lonely. It was pretty out there in the wood, when the snow lay thick and that hare came springing over me; but then I did not like it. It is terribly lonely up here!

Suddenly two little mice crept out. They sniffed at the Fir Tree, and then climbed into its branches.

"It's terribly cold up here," said the two little mice. "Don't you think so, old tree?"

"I'm not old,"
said the Fir Tree.

"Where do
you come from?"
asked the mice.
"And what do you
know?" They were
very inquisitive. "Tell
us about the most
beautiful place in the world! Have you been there?"

"The most beautiful place in the world," said the tree, "is the woods, where the sun shines, and where the birds sing."

And then it told the mice all about its youth.

The little mice listened and said, "What a lot of things you have seen! How happy you must have been!"

"Yes," said the Fir Tree, "those were really quite happy times." But then he told them about the Christmas Eve, when he had been decorated with candy and candles.

"Oh!" said the little mice. "How happy you have been, old tree!"

"I'm not old," said the tree. "I only came out of the wood this winter."

"What splendid stories you can tell!" said the little mice.

And the next night they came with four other little mice, to hear what the tree had to tell.

So the Fir Tree told them the story of Klumpey-Dumpey and the little mice ran right to the very top of the tree with pleasure. Next night, a great many more mice came, and the Fir Tree told the same story again. But when they found out that the tree did not know any other stories the mice grew bored and went away.

The Fir Tree was sad.

"It was very nice when the merry little mice listened to my story, but it will soon be spring now. I shall be so pleased when they take me out of this lonely place."

But when spring came people came and

rummaged in the attic. A servant dragged the tree downstairs where the daylight shone.

Now life is beginning again! thought the tree.

It felt the fresh air and the sunbeams in the courtyard. The courtyard was close to a garden where the roses were in flower, the trees were in full leaf and the swallows were singing.

"Now I shall live!" said the tree joyfully, and spread its branches out; but, alas! They were all withered and yellow; it lay in the corner among nettles and weeds. The tinsel star was still on it, and shone in the bright sunshine.

In the courtyard the children, who had danced around the tree at Christmas, were playing. One of them ran up and tore off the golden star.

"Look what is sticking to the ugly old fir tree," said the child, and he trod upon the branches till they cracked again under his boots.

And the tree looked at all the flowers and the lovely garden, and then looked at itself and wished it had stayed in the dark corner of the attic. It thought of its fresh youth in the wood, of the merry Christmas Eve, and of the little mice who had listened so happily to the story of Klumpey-Dumpey.

"Past! Past!" said the old tree. "It's all over. If only I had been happier at the time."

And a servant came and chopped the tree into little pieces; a whole bundle lay there. It blazed brightly in the stove and it sighed deeply, and each sigh was like a little explosion. The children sat down by the fire, looked into it, and cried, "Snap! Crackle!"

But at each explosion, which was a deep sigh, the tree thought of a summer day in the woods, or of a winter night there when the stars shone. He thought of Christmas Eve and of Klumpey-Dumpey, the only story he had ever heard or knew how to tell; and then the tree was burned.

The children played in the garden, and the youngest put on the golden star which the tree had worn on its happiest evening.

Now that was over, and the tree's life was over, and the story is over too!

THE NIGHTINGALE

This is a story about an emperor of China who was, of course, Chinese. It happened a long time ago, but it's worth telling again so it is not forgotten.

The emperor's palace was the most splendid in the world. It was made entirely of the best porcelain, which was so fragile that one had to be careful at every step. The most wonderful flowers grew in the garden. They were hung with silver bells which rang out when the wind blew. The emperor's garden was so enormous that even the gardener did not know where it ended. Beyond it lay deep lakes and a forest which went right to the sea.

In a tree at the water's edge lived a Nightingale, which sang so beautifully that even the busy fisherman on his way to put out his nets listened to it.

"How beautiful!" he said, each time he heard the bird. "How beautiful!"

Many travelers came from all over the world to visit the city of the emperor, and they admired it very much, and the palace, and the garden, but when they heard the Nightingale, they said, "That is more beautiful than anything else." And when they went home they told everyone what they had seen and some of them wrote books about the Chinese emperor and his city, his palace and his garden; and the ones who were poets wrote fabulous poems about the Nightingale in the woods.

Some of these books found their way to the emperor. He sat in his golden chair and read them from cover to cover. He nodded with pleasure at the excellent descriptions of his city, his palace, and his garden. But when he came to the place where it said: "But the Nightingale is more beautiful than anything else," he was puzzled.

"What's this?" he exclaimed. "I don't know anything at all about the Nightingale. Is there such a bird in my own garden? I've never heard a word about this bird. To think I should have to learn such a thing from a book!"

And he at once sent for his Lord Chamberlain who was very grand and had a very high opinion of himself.

"It says in this book that there is a wonderful bird here called a Nightingale!" said the emperor.

"They say it is the best thing in all my great empire, so why have I never heard anything about it?"

"Only because he has never been invited to the palace," said the Lord Chamberlain, who did not want the emperor to know that he too had never heard of the Nightingale.

"I command that he shall appear this evening, and sing before me," said the emperor. "So go and find him!"

"At once, Your Majesty!" said the Lord Chamberlain. "I will go find him at once!"

But where was he to be found? The Lord Chamberlain ran up and down all the staircases, through halls and passages, but no one had heard of the Nightingale. So he ran back to the emperor, and said that it must have been made up by the writer of the book.

"But the book," said the emperor, "was sent to me by the mighty emperor of Japan, so it cannot be untrue. I will hear the Nightingale! I insist, and I will hear it this very night!"

"Tsing-pe!" said the Lord Chamberlain and again he ran up and down all the staircases, and through all the halls and corridors and this time he met a little kitchen-maid who said: "The Nightingale? Oh yes! It sings beautifully. Every evening I am allowed to take the leftovers to my sick mother. She lives down by the seashore and on my way back I stop for a rest in the woods, and that's when I hear the Nightingale sing. It's so beautiful it always makes me cry!"

"Little kitchen-maid," said the Lord Chamberlain, "if you will lead us to the Nightingale I will get you permission to watch the emperor eating his supper!"

Followed by half the emperor's court the kitchen-maid led the way to the woods. When they were halfway there a cow began to moo.

"Oh!" cried the courtiers. "That's it! That's the Nightingale. Surely we've heard it before."

The little kitchen-maid laughed. "No, those are cows!" she said.

Then the frogs began to croak down by the lake.

"Glorious!" said the courtiers. "It sounds just like church bells."

"No, those are frogs!" laughed the little kitchen-maid. "But now I think we shall soon hear it."

And then the Nightingale began to sing.

"There it is!" said the kitchen-maid and she pointed to a little gray bird up in the boughs of a tree.

"How disappointing!" cried the Lord Chamberlain. "It looks so plain, so dull! It must have lost all its colors at seeing so many important people."

"Little Nightingale!" called the little kitchen-maid. "Our gracious emperor wishes you to sing for him."

"With the greatest pleasure!" replied the Nightingale, thinking that the emperor was there with the others, and began to sing most beautifully.

"No, no, my excellent little Nightingale," said the Lord Chamberlain. "The emperor is not here but in the palace, he has sent me to ask you to come and sing for him there this evening."

"My song sounds best out in the open air!" replied the Nightingale, but it agreed to do what the emperor wished.

That evening the emperor sat on his throne in the palace with a golden perch at his side for the Nightingale. The whole Court was present, and the little kitchen-maid was allowed to stand behind the door. Everyone looked at the little gray bird, and at a nod from the emperor the Nightingale began to sing so beautifully that the Emperor's eyes filled with tears, which poured down his cheeks. And then the Nightingale sang more sweetly still and pierced his heart. He was so pleased that he offered the Nightingale his golden slipper, but the Nightingale said, "Thank you, but I have seen tears

in your eyes and that is the treasure. I am rewarded enough!" And then it sang again with its sweet voice.

From that day the Nightingale lived in the palace. It had its own cage and was allowed to go out once a day accompanied by twelve servants, each of whom held on tightly to a silken string tied to the bird's leg.

The whole city talked of nothing but the wonderful bird, and if two people met, one said, "Nightin," and the other said "gale," and they smiled at one another happily. Eleven children were named after the bird, but not one of them could sing a note and the ladies at Court even put water in their mouths and gurgled when they spoke, hoping that they sounded like the Nightingale.

One day the Emperor received a large parcel, on which was written "The Nightingale."

It contained a box with a clockwork nightingale in it, which could sing like the real one. It was made of gold and silver and brilliantly decorated with diamonds and rubies. As soon as it was wound up its little silver tail went up and down, and it sang just like the real Nightingale. Around his neck hung a little ribbon, and on that was written: "This gift from the emperor of Japan is a poor toy compared with the emperor of China's real bird."

"Oh no!" said everyone. "It's lovely! They must sing together!"

And so the two birds had to sing together; but it did not sound very nice, for the real Nightingale sang in its own way, and the clockwork nightingale sang dance tunes. But when the clockwork bird

sang by itself it sounded just as good as the real one, and with all those jewels was much prettier to look at. It sang the same song more than thirty-three times but was not tired. The courtiers would have been happy to go on listening to it but the emperor said, "No! It's time for the real Nightingale to sing something now."

But where was it? No one had noticed that it had flown away out of the open window, back to the green woods that were his home.

"Ungrateful bird!" said the emperor.

"Never mind," said the courtiers. "The clock-work bird is better and prettier."

So the emperor banished the real Nightingale from the empire, and put the clockwork bird on a silken cushion next to his bed.

A whole year went by. The emperor, the Court, and all the people in China knew every little twitter of the clockwork bird's song by heart.

But one evening, when it was singing at its best, something inside the bird broke. It whirred and went "Ping!" and the music suddenly stopped.

The emperor jumped out of bed and sent for his doctor, but what could he do? Then they sent for a watchmaker who, after poking about, said that the bird must be carefully treated, for the clockwork pieces were wearing out and it would be impossible to put in new ones. He said the bird could only sing once a year and even that was one time too many.

Five years went by, and the emperor fell ill. He was not expected to live much longer. He lay cold and pale in his magnificent bed with its long velvet curtains and heavy gold tassels. The window was open, and the moon shone in upon the emperor and the clockwork bird.

The poor emperor opened his eyes, and he saw Death standing at the foot of his bed wearing his

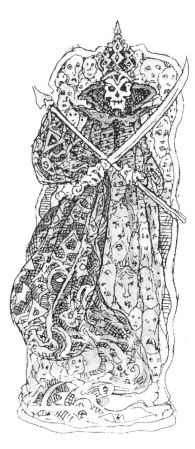

golden crown, and holding his sword, and in the other his beautiful banner. Around him floated strange shadowy faces. These were all the emperor's bad and good deeds whispering to him about his past.

"Do you remember this?" they whispered. "Do you remember that?"

The emperor shivered and shook.

"Music!" he cried out. "Let me have music so that I cannot hear what they are saying!"

"Sing!" cried the emperor. "You little precious golden bird, sing, sing!"

But the bird was silent on its golden perch. No one was there to wind him up. Then suddenly through the window came the most beautiful song. It was the real Nightingale sitting on the branch of a tree. It had heard that the emperor was dying and had come to sing to him of comfort and hope. And as it sang the shadowy faces grew paler and paler, and the emperor began to feel stronger. Even Death himself listened, and said: "Don't stop little Nightingale, don't stop!"

"I'll go on singing if you give me that splendid golden sword, the banner, and the emperor's crown!"

And Death gave up each of these treasures for the love of the Nightingale's song. And the Nightingale sang on and on. It sang of the quiet churchyard where the white roses grow and where the elder blossom smells sweet, and where the grass is wet from the tears of those who mourn. All at once Death felt a longing to see his garden and floated out of the window in the form of a cold white mist.

"Thank you! Thank you!" said the emperor. "You heavenly little bird! I know you well. I banished you from my empire, and yet you have charmed and banished Death himself! How can I reward you?"

"You have rewarded me!" replied the Nightingale. "I drew tears from your eyes when I sang the first time—I shall never forget that. Those are the jewels that rejoice a singer's heart. But now you must sleep and grow strong again. I will sing you a lullaby."

And it sang, and the emperor fell into a sweet deep sleep. The sun was shining on him through the window when he awoke, completely well again. He was all alone as everyone thought he was dead. Only the Nightingale still sat beside him and sang.

"You must always stay with me now," said the emperor, "and I shall break the clockwork bird into a thousand pieces."

"No! No!" replied the Nightingale. "It did what it could. Keep it and let me come when I feel the wish. Then I will sit in the evening on that branch by the window and sing of those who are happy and of those who suffer. I will sing of all the good and of evil that you cannot see. A little singing bird can fly all over your empire and listen to the poorest fisherman and the richest farmer. I will come and sing to you and tell you all I hear—but one thing you must promise me."

"Anything!" said the emperor, standing there once more in his imperial robes with his gold sword at his side.

"Never tell anyone that you have a little bird who tells you everything." And the Nightingale flew away.

The servants came in expecting to see their emperor lying dead, but there he stood, alive and well. He turned to them with a smile and said, "Good morning!"

THE SWINEHERD

There was once a poor prince who was in love with the emperor's daughter and wanted to marry her. But what could he give her? His kingdom was very small and he had no gold. But he did have a rosebush, a beautiful, magical rosebush which bloomed only every five years, and even then bore only a single rose, but what a rose! Its scent was so sweet that whoever smelled it forgot all sorrow and trouble. The prince also had a nightingale, which could sing every song in the world. The prince loved the emperor's daughter so much that he sent her his rose and his nightingale in two silver caskets.

The emperor ordered the presents to be brought into the great hall where the princess was playing with her friends. When she saw the great silver caskets with the presents in them, she said: "Oh, I do hope they are kittens!"

But out came the rosebush with the beautiful rose.

"Now isn't that pretty!" said the emperor.

But the Princess touched the rose and then she began to cry.

"Ugh! But it's not made of silk! It's a real rose!" she said. "It's a real rose!"

"Let us first see what is in the other casket before we get angry," said the emperor. And he took the nightingale out. It sang so beautifully that at first no one could think of anything bad to say about it.

"Oh, I do hope it is not a real bird," said the princess.

"But it is a real bird," said the emperor.

"Then let it fly away," said the princess rudely, "and tell the prince I don't like his presents and I certainly won't marry him."

But the prince was not discouraged. He disguised himself in ragged clothes, pulled his hat down low, and knocked at the castle door.

"Good day," he said to the emperor. "I would like to work for you."

"It just so happens that I need someone who can look after my pigs," the emperor replied.

So the prince became the emperor's swineherd and was given a wretched little room down by the pigsty. All day long he looked after the pigs but at night he made a pretty little pot, with bells all around it. When the pot boiled the bells rang out and played the old song:

Oh, my darling Augustine,
All is lost, all is lost.

But the best thing about the little pot was that if you held your finger over it, you could at once smell what was cooking on every stove in town.

One day the princess was out walking near the pigsty. She saw the pot and heard it singing.

"I know that tune!" she said. "I can play it on my piano." And she ordered her servant to go and ask the swineherd how much the pot cost.

"How much is the pot?" the servant asked the swineherd.

"I will sell it to the princess if she gives me ten kisses," replied the swineherd.

The servant was shocked and ran back to the princess.

"Well," said the princess, "what did he say?"

"I don't like to say it out loud," replied the servant.

"Well, whisper it in my ear," said the princess. So the servant whispered in her ear.

"He is very rude," said the princess, "but I do so

want that pot. Go back and ask him if he will take ten kisses from you, instead of me!"

"Sorry," replied the swineherd. "It's ten kisses from the princess or I keep my pot."

"Isn't he tiresome?" said the princess to her servant. "Well, go on then! Stand behind me so that nobody can see me!"

So the servant stood behind and spread out her apron, and then the princess gave the swineherd ten kisses, and the swineherd gave her the pot.

Back at the castle the pot was kept boiling day and night. The princess was delighted. "Now I know who is having soup and pancakes for dinner," she said, "and who is having plum pudding and cutlets! I can smell them all."

The swineherd, that is to say, the prince, looked after the pigs very well but let no day pass by without making something. Next he made a rattle, and when he swung this rattle it played all the dances that have been known since the world began.

"But that is wonderful!" cried the princess, as she went past the pigsty. "Go down and ask how much it costs," she said to her servant, "but I'm not giving him any more kisses."

"This time he says he must have a hundred kisses," said the servant when she came back.

"He's crazy!" exclaimed the princess, and she walked off. But when she had gone a little distance she stopped and said to herself, I am the emperor's daughter and I want that rattle! I'll give him ten kisses, like last time, and he can take the rest from my servant.

But the servant came back with the same message: "A hundred kisses from the princess or I keep the rattle."

"Oh well then!" sighed the princess to her servant. "Stand behind me again!"

And once more the servant stood behind the princess while she kissed the swineherd.

"What is that crowd down by the pigsty?" asked the emperor, who had stepped out onto his balcony. He rubbed his eyes and put on his spectacles. "Why, there's my own daughter and that silly young servant-girl up to some mischief! I shall have to go down to them."

And he put on his slippers and hurried down to the pigsty. He went so quietly, and the princess, the servant, and the swineherd were so busy counting kisses that they did not hear him coming.

When the emperor saw what was going on he was so angry he whacked them all and threw them out of his kingdom.

The princess stood outside the city gates in the pouring rain and wept.

"Oh, what a fool I've been," she cried. "If only I had married the handsome prince!"

Then the swineherd went behind a tree, washed his face, took off his rags, and stepped out in his prince's clothes. He looked so good and handsome that the princess curtsied to him.

"I loved you once," said the prince, "but not any more. You did not want me. You thought nothing of the lovely rose and the sweet nightingale, yet you were ready to kiss a swineherd for a cooking-pot and a rattle. And now you have got what you deserve!"

Then he turned his back on the princess and returned to his own kingdom.

So the princess was left alone in the rain with the old song ringing in her ears:

Oh, my darling Augustine,
All is lost, all is lost.

THUMBELINA

There was once a woman who longed to have a tiny little child, but she did not know where to find one. So she went to an old witch and said: "I do so much wish for a tiny little child! Can you not tell me where I can get one?"

"Oh, that's easy!" said the witch. "Take this magic grain of barley home put it in a flowerpot, and you shall see what you shall see."

"Thank you," said the woman. She gave the witch a silver shilling, went home, and planted the magic seed. Before she could turn around a big handsome flower sprang up. It looked like a tulip, but the leaves were tightly closed, as though it were still a bud.

"What a beautiful flower," said the woman, and she kissed its red and yellow petals, and, as she kissed it, the flower opened. There, in the middle of the flower, sitting on a green velvet stool, was a lovely little girl no bigger than the woman's thumb, so she called her Thumbelina.

At night Thumbelina slept in a polished walnut shell with violet petals for her mattress and a rose petal for a blanket. In the daytime she played on the table, where the woman had put a bowl of water with flowers around it and a big tulip leaf floating in it. Thumbelina pretended the leaf was a boat and rowed from one side of the bowl to the other, using two horsehairs for oars. She was so happy playing there that she sang to her heart's content.

But one night as she lay asleep in her pretty bed, an old toad came creeping through a broken windowpane. The toad was very ugly, big, and damp. It hopped straight down onto the table where Thumbelina lay sleeping under the rose petal.

"She would make a lovely wife for my son," said the toad. So she took the walnut shell in which Thumbelina was fast asleep and hopped away through the window down to the river where she lived with her son, who was even uglier than his mother.

"Don't wake her up yet," said the old toad to her son. "She might run away from us. We will put her out on the river on one of the broad water lily leaves, then she won't be able to get away, while we get your wedding feast ready."

There were many water lilies with broad green leaves on the river. The old toad swam out to the biggest one and laid the walnut shell on it. When little Thumbelina woke up and saw where she was, she began to cry very bitterly; for there was water on every side of the great green leaf, and there was no way for her to reach dry land.

The old toad swam out with her ugly son to visit Thumbelina.

"Here is my son," she croaked. "He will be your husband, and you will live happily together on the riverbank."

Then they took Thumbelina's little bed away to put it in the bedroom they were getting ready for her, and Thumbelina sat all alone upon the green leaf and wept, for she did not want to have the old toad's ugly son for a husband.

The fish swimming in the water below had seen

the toad and had also heard what she said, so they peeped out to look at Thumbelina. When they saw how little and pretty she was, they felt so sorry for her that they all gathered around the green stalk which held the leaf on which she was sitting and gnawed at it until it snapped off and floated down the river. Away went Thumbelina, far far away where the toads could not get at her.

For many days Thumbelina sailed down the river. The sun shone on the water which glistened like gold. She was so happy to be safe from the toads that she felt like singing.

But suddenly a big beetle flew down, snatched her up and flew with her up into a tree, where he sat down with her on a big green leaf and gave her some honeydew to drink.

"You are very pretty," he said, "even if you are not a beetle," and he invited all the other beetles who lived in the tree to come and see Thumbelina.

The beetles stared at her and said: "But she's only got two legs and no feelers! Ugh! She looks like one of those ugly human creatures!"

Of course Thumbelina was very pretty. Even the beetle who had carried her off saw that; but when all the other beetles said she was ugly, he thought it wiser to agree with them. He flew down with her from the tree and put her on a daisy, and Thumbelina wept, because she believed what the beetles had said.

All that summer poor Thumbelina lived alone in the great woods. She wove herself a bed out of blades of grass, and hung it up under a shamrock leaf to protect herself from the rain. She sipped the honey from the flowers for food and drank the morning dew out of the leaves. Summer and fall came and went and then it was winter. All the birds flew away. Trees and flowers shed their leaves. The great shamrock under which she had lived shriveled to a withered yellow stalk. She was dreadfully cold, for her clothes were in rags.

Poor little Thumbelina! She nearly froze to death. It began to snow, and every snowflake that fell upon her was like a whole shovelful thrown upon one of us; for we are tall, and she was only an inch high. So she wrapped herself in a dry leaf and set out across a big cornfield.

The stiff cold stubble was like a forest for her to struggle through. But at last she arrived, shivering with cold, at the door of a field mouse. This mouse lived in a warm and comfortable hole with a big storeroom full of corn. Poor Thumbelina knocked at the door and begged for a grain of wheat because she had not had anything to eat for two days.

"You poor little girl," said the field mouse, for she was a kind old field mouse, "come into my warm house at once and have something to eat."

The field mouse liked Thumbelina and said, "You can stay with me for the winter, if you keep my house clean and neat and tell me little stories in the evening."

And Thumbelina did what the kind old field mouse asked of her, and was very comfortable and happy.

One day the field mouse said, "My neighbor the mole is coming to visit me." When the mole came in his black velvet coat the field mouse asked Thumbelina to sing for them after supper. When the mole heard her lovely voice he fell in love with Thumbelina and decided that one day he would marry her. He invited Thumbelina and the field mouse to come and see the long tunnel he had just dug between his house and theirs.

He led the way through the long dark tunnel until suddenly he stopped and thrust his broad nose through the ceiling, and made a big hole. By the daylight shining in Thumbelina saw a dead swallow lying there. His beautiful wings were pressed close against his sides, and his head and feet tucked under his feathers.

Poor bird, thought Thumbelina, he has died of cold as I nearly did. She felt very sorry for the swallow, but the mole prodded him with a short strong leg, and said, "He can't sing anymore. It must be miserable to be born a little bird. I'm glad none of my children will ever be a bird with nothing to do except sing 'tweet-weet,' and then die of hunger in winter!"

"I quite agree, you wise man," said the field mouse. "I've never understood all the fuss about birds."

Thumbelina said nothing; but when the others weren't looking she bent down and kissed the bird on his closed eyes.

The mole closed up the hole through which the daylight shone in, and they all went home. But that night Thumbelina could not sleep so she got up and wove a large blanket of hay, crept back through the tunnel, and spread it over the dead bird.

"Good-bye, you pretty little bird!" she said, "good-bye," and then she gently laid her head on the bird's breast. But the bird was not dead; he was lying there numb with cold and now he had been warmed, his heart began to beat more strongly.

Thumbelina was so startled that she trembled; the bird was large, very large compared with her. But she took courage and tucked the hay blanket closer around the poor bird.

The next night she crept out to him again. He was alive but very weak. He opened his eyes for a moment and looked at Thumbelina.

"Thank you, you pretty little child," said the swallow. "I feel much warmer now. I shall get my strength back again soon, and then I shall be able to fly about in the warm sunshine."

"Oh no!" said Thumbelina, "it is still winter out there. It is snowing and bitterly cold. Stay in your warm bed and I will look after you."

All winter the swallow stayed there in the tunnel, and Thumbelina came every day with water in a flower petal and grains of wheat from the field mouse's store. The field mouse and the mole never found out what Thumbelina was doing, because they no longer used the tunnel.

When spring came the swallow was well again and ready to leave. Thumbelina opened the hole which the mole had made in the ceiling. The sun shone in on them.

"Come with me!" said the swallow. "You can sit on my back and we will fly away."

But Thumbelina knew that the old field mouse would be upset if she left her. "No, dear swallow, I cannot go with you," said Thumbelina.

"Then good-bye, good-bye, you good, pretty little girl!" said the swallow; and he flew out into the sunshine. Thumbelina watched him go with tears in her eyes for she dearly loved the swallow.

Thumbelina felt very sad and even sadder when the field mouse said, "It's time now to get ready to marry the mole, Thumbelina."

The mole hired four spiders to make Thumbelina's wedding dress and every evening he paid her a visit. He hated the summer and decided that the wedding would not take place till the fall. Thumbelina did not like the mole at all. Every morning when the sun rose and every evening when it set, she stood at the door and wished with all her heart that she could see her dear swallow again. But the swallow did not come back; he had flown far away. Fall came and Thumbelina's wedding dress was ready. But Thumbelina wept and told the field mouse she did not want to marry the tiresome mole.

"Nonsense," said the field mouse, "he is a very fine mole. You are very lucky."

On the wedding day the mole came to fetch Thumbelina. Now she would have to live with him deep under the earth and never come out into the warm sunshine, for the mole did not like the sun. Thumbelina was very sorrowful. For one last time she stood at the field mouse's door saying good-bye to the sun and the flowers when suddenly she heard a bird singing.

She looked up and saw the swallow flying by. The swallow was overjoyed to see Thumbelina. She told him how unwilling she was to marry the mole and live deep under the earth where the sun never shone. She burst into tears.

"The cold winter is coming now," said the swallow. "I am going to fly far away to a warm country. Come with me! You can sit on my back and we will fly away from the mole and his dark room, far away, over the mountains to a warm country where it is always summer. Oh come with me, dear little Thumbelina. After all, you saved my life when I lay frozen in the dark tunnel."

"Yes, I will go with you!" said Thumbelina, and she climbed onto the bird's back and tied her sash to

one of his strongest feathers. Then the swallow flew up into the air over forest and over sea, high up over the mountains where the snow always lies. It was cold up there, but the swallow's feathers kept Thumbelina warm.

At last they came to a land where the sun was very hot and the sky seemed twice as high. There were vineyards full of blue and green grapes and little trees covered with oranges and lemons. But the swallow flew on until they came to an even lovelier place. Under glorious green trees by a blue lake stood a palace of dazzling white marble. There were many swallows' nests on the roof of the palace. But the swallow said, "My nest is here but it is not the right kind of house for you, Thumbelina," and he flew down into the garden with Thumbelina and set her upon the broad leaf of a beautiful white flower.

To Thumbelina's surprise, who should be sitting there but a little man no bigger than herself. He was as crystal clear as glass and wore a pretty gold

crown on his head, and bright wings on his shoulders. He was the king of the flower fairies.

"How beautiful he is!" whispered Thumbelina to the swallow.

The little king was rather frightened of the swallow, who looked gigantic to him. But he thought that Thumbelina was the prettiest little girl he had ever seen. He took off his golden crown, and put it on her, and asked Thumbelina if she would be his wife and queen of all the flowers.

Thumbelina had fallen in love with the little king as soon as she saw him, so she said, "Yes." And at once out of every flower came a fairy. Each one brought Thumbelina a present, but the best gift was a pair of beautiful wings so she could fly from flower to flower.

The swallow sang at the wedding and came to see Thumbelina every day. He was sad when the time came for him to fly back to Denmark. But there he made his nest over the window of the man who is telling you these fairy tales, and there he told that man this story.

THE LITTLE MATCH GIRL

It was snowing heavily and already getting dark on the last evening of the year. In the icy wind a poor little girl, bareheaded and barefoot, was walking through the streets. When she left her own house she had been wearing slippers, but they were too big for her and they had come off as she ran across the road where a carriage had nearly knocked her down. So now the little girl went barefoot. She was carrying a bundle of matches in her hand. No one had bought any from her all day, and no one had given her so much as a penny.

Shivering with cold and hunger she crept along, her long hair covered in snowflakes, a picture of misery, poor little girl! Lights shone from all the windows and there was a glorious smell of roast goose in the air, for it was New Year's Eve.

She sat down cowering in a corner between two

houses and tucked her little feet beneath her, but she was still as cold as ever. She did not dare go home, because she had not sold any matches and she knew her father would beat her for that.

Her little hands were numb with the cold. Perhaps a lighted match would warm her up, if she could only pull one from the bundle and strike it against the wall. She pulled one out. Scratch! How it spluttered and burned! It was a warm, bright flame, like a candle. The little girl dreamed that she was sitting in front of a big warm polished stove, with a warm bright glow. How the fire burned! How comfortable it was! And then the little flame went out, the stove vanished, and all that was left was the burned-out match in her hand.

She struck a second match against the wall. By the light of its flame she thought she could see into a room with a table covered in a snow–white cloth and laid with beautiful china. She could see a steaming hot roast goose stuffed with chestnuts and apples. And suddenly the goose hopped down from the dish and waddled along the floor, with a knife and fork in its breast straight to the little girl. Then the match went out, and she was once more out in the bitter cold. She lit another match and dreamed she was sitting under a beautiful Christmas tree, far bigger and far more beautiful than any she had seen in any window. Thousands of candles burned on its green branches and it was covered in the loveliest decorations. The little girl stretched out her hand toward them and then the match went out. But, as it did so, the little girl saw the lights from the Christmas tree shoot up into the sky and turn into stars. And then, as she watched, the brightest star fell back to earth.

Someone, somewhere is dying, thought the little girl. Grandmother told me that just before she died. She told me that whenever a star falls to earth a soul goes back to heaven.

She struck another match against the wall and by its light the little girl saw her beloved grandmother standing there, bright and shining, looking at her with love and pity in her eyes.

"Oh, Grandmother!"
cried the child. "Take me with you!
I know you will go when the match is burned out.
You will vanish like the warm fire, the warm food,
and the wonderful Christmas tree!"

And she quickly struck all the matches on the
wall because she wanted to keep her grandmother
with her. And the matches burned with such a
glow that night turned into day. Never had the
grandmother looked so beautiful. She took the

little girl in her arms, and both flew in brightness and joy up above the earth, very, very high up where there was neither cold, nor hunger, nor care.

On New Year's Day the child was found frozen to death with all the matches used up. She lay there, covered in snow but with a sweet smile on her face.

"The poor, poor child," the people said. "She must have been trying to keep warm."

They had no idea what beautiful things the little match girl had seen before her soul went quietly and happily away with her grandmother on New Year's Day.

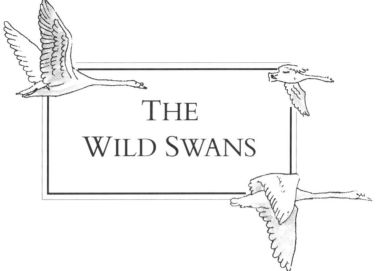

THE WILD SWANS

Far, far away, where the swallows fly when our winter comes, lived a king who had eleven sons and one daughter, named Eliza. The eleven princes each went to school with a star on his breast and a sword by his side. They wrote with pencils of diamond upon slates of gold. Their sister Eliza sat on a little glass stool and had a picture book which had cost as much as half a kingdom.

How rich and happy they were! But this did not last.

Their father, the king, married a wicked queen who did not love the children at all. On the very first day they noticed this. There was great feasting in the palace, but instead of being given all the spare cake and fruit, as usual, they were just given some sand in a teacup and told to pretend that it was something good to eat.

A week later the queen took little Eliza into the country, to a peasant and his wife, and before long she was telling the king so many lies about the poor princes that he did not bother with them anymore.

"Fly out into the world and look after yourselves," said the wicked queen to the princes. "Fly like great birds without voices."

But she could not make it as bad for them as she wished, for they turned into eleven magnificent wild swans. With a strange cry they flew out of the palace windows, over the park into the woods.

It was still quite early morning when they passed over the place where their sister Eliza lay asleep in the peasant's hut. They hovered over the roof, craned their long necks, and beat their huge wings, but no one heard them. They had to fly on, high up and far away into the wide world. There they flew into a great dark forest which stretched away to the seashore.

Little Eliza had nothing to play with except a green leaf. She pricked a hole in the leaf and looked through it up at the sun. It seemed to her that she could see her brothers' clear eyes, and each time the sunbeams warmed her cheeks, she thought of all the kisses they had given her.

When Eliza was fifteen years old, she was sent home, and when the queen saw how beautiful she was, she hated her. She longed to change her into a wild swan, like her brothers, but she did not dare to because the king wished to see his daughter.

The queen fetched three toads and took them into the bathroom, which was built of marble and decorated with cushions and fine rugs. She kissed the toads and said to the first: "Sit on Eliza's head when she gets into the bath, so that she will become as stupid as you. Sit on her forehead," she said to the second, "so she will become as ugly as you, and her father will not recognize her. Rest on her heart," she whispered to the third, "so that she becomes evil and suffers pain from it."

She put the toads into the clear water, which at once turned green, and calling Eliza, told her to undress and get into the bath. The toads sat on Eliza's hair, her forehead, and her heart, but she did not seem to notice them, and when she stood up, three red poppies were floating on the water. Eliza was too good and innocent for evil sorcery to have any power over her.

When the wicked queen saw that, she rubbed Eliza's skin with walnut juice, and smeared a painful ointment on her face, and tangled her beautiful hair into such a mess that her father simply did not recognize her. Only the dogs and the swallows still knew who she was, but of course they could not say anything.

Sadly Eliza crept out of the castle and walked all day till she came to the great forest. She did not know where to go. She only knew that she longed for her brothers and that she would look for them everywhere until she found them.

When night fell, she lay down on the soft moss and fell asleep. All night long she dreamed of her brothers. They were children again playing together, and looking at her beautiful picture book which had cost half a kingdom. In the dream everything in the picture book came to life: the birds sang, and the people came out of the book and spoke to Eliza and her brothers.

When she awoke the sun was already up and she could hear the sound of running water. It was coming from a stream flowing into a lake. The lake was as clear as a mirror, and when Eliza saw her face in it she was horrified to see how ugly and dirty she was.

First she washed her face. Then she undressed and bathed in the water till once again she was beautiful. She dried herself and got dressed, braided her long hair, and drank some water from the sparkling stream. Then she set off into the dark forest.

She had been wandering there a long time when she saw an old woman coming toward her. She had berries in her basket and she gave some to Eliza.

"Have you seen eleven princes riding through here?" Eliza asked the old woman.

"No, my dear," said the old woman, "but yesterday

I saw eleven swans swimming in the river over there, and they had golden crowns on their heads."

And she led Eliza to a hill at the bottom of which a little river wound its way. Eliza said good-bye to the old woman and followed the river down to the seashore.

The great, empty ocean lay before her eyes. What was she to do now? She looked at the count-less little pebbles on the shore, worn smooth by the sea.

The sea is never tired of rolling in and rolling out, thought Eliza, and I must never get tired of looking for my brothers.

On the foam-covered seaweed lay eleven white swan feathers. Eliza gathered them together as if they were flowers. Drops of water were upon them, but who knows if they were dewdrops or tears? It was lonely on that beach, but Eliza stayed there and watched the wind playing with the waves, and listened to the murmur of the sea.

Just as the sun was setting Eliza saw eleven wild swans, with crowns on their heads, flying toward the land. They swept along one after the other like a long white ribbon. Eliza hid behind a bush. The swans landed near her and flapped their great white wings.

The very minute the sun set the swans' feathers fell off, and eleven handsome princes, Eliza's brothers, stood there. She cried out and flung herself into their arms and called them by their names. How happy the princes were to see their little sister again, now grown so tall and beautiful. They laughed and cried together, and soon found out how cruel their stepmother had been to them all.

"We brothers," said the eldest, "fly about as wild swans as long as the sun is in the sky, but as soon as it starts to set we turn into humans again. So we must always be sure to have a safe landing-ground when the sun sets. If at that moment we were still flying up toward the clouds, we would fall to our death. We do not live here but in a beautiful land beyond the sea. It is a very long journey. We have to cross the ocean and the only place where we can spend the night is on a little rock in the middle

of it. There we spend the night in our human form—without this rock we could never visit our beloved homeland. We are only allowed to visit our home once a year. For eleven days we may stay here and fly over the great forest. From there we can see the palace in which we were born and in which our father lives, and the churchyard where our mother lies buried. And now we have found you, dear little sister! But we must leave in two days. We want to take you with us, Eliza, but how can we do it as swans and without a boat?"

"And how can I free you from the spell?" asked Eliza.

They talked long into the night, but they fell asleep without finding any answers to their questions.

The rustling of wings woke Eliza. Her brothers were swans again and were flying away, all except the youngest, who stayed behind and laid his head

in her lap. Eliza stroked his wings. They stayed together all day. Toward evening the others came back, and when the sun had set there they stood in human form once more.

"Tomorrow we fly far away from here and can not come back for a whole year. But we can not leave you here! Have you the courage to come with us? Our wings are strong enough to carry you over the sea."

"Yes! Take me with you," said Eliza.

All night long they wove a net of willow bark and tough reeds. Eliza lay down on this strong net and when the sun rose, and her brothers had changed into wild swans, they seized it in their beaks, and flew with their beloved sister, who had fallen asleep, high up toward the clouds. The youngest swan always flew over her head to keep the sun out of her eyes.

They were far from the shore when Eliza awoke.

By her side lay some ripe berries. The youngest swan had collected them for her. All day they flew on but their flight was slower than usual because they were carrying their sister. Eliza looked for the little rock in the ocean, but it was nowhere to be seen. It was her fault the swans could not fly any faster! When the sun went down they would turn into men and fall into the sea and drown.

And now the sun was dipping into the sea. Eliza trembled. Then suddenly the swans darted down-ward. At last Eliza saw the little rock beneath her. It looked no larger than a seal might look, thrusting his head out of the water. The sun was sinking fast as her foot touched the firm land. Her brothers were standing around her, arm in arm. There was just enough room for them all. The sea thundered against the rock and drenched them with spray but Eliza and her brothers held hands and sang songs to keep up their courage.

At daybreak the storm died down, and when the

148

sun rose the swans flew away with Eliza. Eliza saw a mountainous country floating in the air beneath her. A fabulous palace rose up surrounded by palm trees and gaudy flowers as big as saucers.

"That is Fata Morgana's palace," her youngest brother told her. "But no human can ever go there."

All day Eliza looked down on the ever-changing scene beneath her, until they came to the real land of blue mountains, forests, and cities where her brothers lived. They set her down outside a great cave hidden by trailing green leaves.

"Now we shall see what you will dream of here tonight," said the youngest brother.

"I hope I will dream of a way to set you free," Eliza replied. And she fell asleep wondering, as always, how she could break the terrible spell.

That night Eliza dreamed that she was flying high in the air to the cloudy palace of Fata Morgana who came out to meet her. She was beautiful and radiant, and yet she looked quite like the old woman who had given her the berries in the wood and had told her about the swans with golden crowns on their heads.

"You can free your brothers," she said. "But have you the courage and perseverance? Do you see this stinging nettle in my hand? Many of the same kind grow around the cave in which you sleep. Remember, only those nettles and those that grow in churchyards are any good. Those are the ones you must pick even if they burn your hands to blisters. Trample these nettles into pieces with your feet, and you will have thread. Then you must spin and weave eleven shirts with long sleeves. Throw these over the eleven swans and the spell will be broken. But don't forget! From the moment you begin this work until it is finished, even if it takes years to complete, you must not speak. The first word you utter will pierce your brothers' hearts like a dagger. Their lives depend on your silence. Remember all this!"

Then she touched Eliza's hand with the nettle. It felt as if her hand was on fire and the pain woke her up. It was broad daylight, and nearby she saw a nettle like the one she had seen in her dream. She went out of the cave and began to pick the ugly nettles. They stung like fire, burning great blisters on her arms and hands, but Eliza thought she could bear the pain if she could only set her brothers

free. Then she trampled on the nettles with her bare feet and spun the green thread.

At sunset her brothers came back. They were frightened by her silence, but when they saw her hands, they understood what she was doing for their sake. The youngest brother wept, and where his tears fell she felt no more pain and all the burning blisters vanished.

Eliza worked all night. She could not sleep until she had set her brothers free. All next day, while the swans were away, she worked on. She had finished one shirt and begun on the second when suddenly she heard the sound of a hunting horn. The noise came nearer and nearer. She heard hounds barking and rushed into the cave. She tied the nettles into a bundle and sat on it.

A huge dog came bounding out of the woods, and then another, and another. They barked loudly, running backward and forward until the huntsmen appeared.

The most handsome of them was the king of the land himself. He gazed and gazed at Eliza. He had never seen such a beautiful girl.

"How did you get here?" he asked.

Eliza shook her head and hid her hands under her apron, so that the king could not see what she was suffering.

"Come with me," he said. "You cannot stay here. If you are as good as you are beautiful, I will dress you in velvet and silk, and crown you as my queen."

Then he lifted her onto his horse. Eliza wept and wrung her hands, but the king said: "I only wish for your happiness: one day you will thank me for this."

And then he galloped away over the mountains with Eliza on his horse, the hunters galloping behind them.

When they reached the king's city he led her into his lovely palace. But Eliza had no eyes for the marble halls and the fountains. She just wept silently as the servants dressed her in rich robes, threaded pearls into her hair, and covered her blistered hands with fine soft gloves.

152

Everyone was dazzled by her beauty, and the king chose her for his bride. But the archbishop shook his head and was heard to mutter: "The girl is almost certainly a witch who has put a spell on our king."

But the king took no notice. "Let there be music!" he ordered, "and dancing and feasting!" And he led Eliza through his sweet-smelling gardens and showed her all his treasures but she never once smiled. Then the king took her to a little room hung with rich green tapestry. It looked exactly like the cave where the king had found her. On the floor lay her precious bundle of nettles and over a chair hung the shirt she had finished.

"Here is the work you were doing when we met," said the king kindly. "You can go on with it here if it makes you happy."

Eliza smiled with joy. Perhaps she could still free her brothers! She kissed the king's hand and he took her gently in his arms. Then he ordered all the church bells to be rung to announce their wedding. And the beautiful dumb girl out of the woods became queen of the country.

All through the wedding ceremony the archbishop whispered evil words into the king's ear, but they did not sink into the king's heart. When it was time to crown Eliza, the archbishop cruelly pressed the heavy crown down so hard on her head that it hurt her. But she bore the pain in silence and smiled at the king. She loved the kind, handsome man who did everything he could to make her happy. As the days went by, she grew to love him more and more. How she wished she could break her silence and tell him everything. But she could not, and every night she crept away from his side, and went quietly to the little room and wove one shirt after another. But when she began the seventh she had no more nettles left.

She knew that there were nettles growing in the churchyard that she could use, but she must pick them herself. With a trembling heart, she crept into the garden in the moonlit night, and went through the deserted streets to the churchyard. There she saw a circle of hideous creatures staring at her with evil eyes. They tried to claw at her with their skinny fingers, but Eliza managed to get past them and collect the stinging nettles and carry them back to the palace.

But the archbishop had seen her. Now he was sure that the queen was a witch. In secret he told the king what he had seen and what he feared. Two heavy tears rolled down the king's cheeks. Every night he pretended to be asleep, but when Eliza got up he followed her quietly and saw her creep into the little green room.

Eliza saw the king's face grow sad and angry. It frightened her, but she did not understand the reason. She had almost finished her work. Ten shirts

were ready but she had no more nettles left. Once more, for the last time, she knew she must go to the churchyard to pick a few more. She was terrified of going there again and of the horrible creatures, but of course she went, and the king and the archbishop followed her. They saw her vanish into the churchyard, and when they drew near, they too saw those evil creatures sitting on the gravestones. The king thought that Eliza had come to visit them and that broke his heart.

"Your queen is a witch," he said to the people the next day. "What shall I do with her?"

"Burn her!" they cried. "Burn her at the stake!"

Eliza was taken from the palace and led into a dark damp cell, where the wind whistled through the grated window. She was given the bundle of nettles which she had collected for her pillow and the burning shirts as a blanket. Nothing could have pleased her more. She picked up the last shirt and went on with her work.

That evening there came the whirling of swans' wings close by the bars of the window. It was the youngest of her brothers. He had found his sister and she cried for joy, even though she knew that the coming night was probably her last. But now her work was almost finished, and her brothers were here.

As soon as the sun rose next morning the eleven brothers came to the palace gate, and demanded to be brought before the king. They were told that the king was still asleep and could not be disturbed. They begged and threatened until the king himself came out and asked what was the meaning of this. At that moment the sun rose, and the brothers were no longer to be seen, but instead eleven wild swans were seen flying away over the palace.

All the people came flocking out at the town gate, for they wanted to see the witch burned. An old horse drew the cart in which Eliza sat. She was dressed in rags and her cheeks were as pale as death. Ten finished shirts lay at her feet and she went on sewing, sewing the last one, the eleventh one.

The crowd pressed around her, jeering and trying to tear up the shirts.

Suddenly eleven wild swans came flying down and sat around her on the cart, and beat their great wings. The crowd fell back in terror.

"Is this a sign from heaven?" they began to whisper. "Perhaps she isn't a witch after all."

The executioner seized hold of her, but then Eliza quickly threw the eleven shirts over the swans, and immediately eleven handsome princes stood there. But the youngest still had one swan's wing instead of an arm, because she had not quite had time to finish the second sleeve.

"Now I may speak!" cried Eliza. "I am no witch!"

Then she sank into her brothers' arms, exhausted by all her work and the pain she had suffered.

"She is indeed innocent," said the eldest brother.

And he told the king and the people the whole story. While he spoke all the wood piled there to burn Eliza began to send out green shoots and the air was filled with the scent of roses. Then a great hedge sprang up covered with red roses and at the top a white starry flower appeared.

The king picked this special flower and laid it on Eliza's heart. Then she woke up with a heart full of peace and joy.

The church bells began ringing by themselves and all the birds began to sing. Everyone cheered as the king and her brothers led Eliza back to the palace where she lived with them all happily ever after.

Biblical Foundation 6

Freedom From The Curse

by Larry Kreider

House To House Publications
Lititz, Pennsylvania USA

Freedom From The Curse

Larry Kreider

Updated Edition © 2002, Reprinted 2003, 2005
Copyright © 1993, 1997, 1999
House to House Publications
11 Toll Gate Road, Lititz, PA 17543
Telephone: 800.848.5892
Web site: www.dcfi.org

ISBN 1-886973-05-9
Design and illustrations by Sarah Sauder

Biblical Foundations

C O N T E N T S

Books in this Series

This is the sixth book in a twelve-book series designed to help believers to build a solid biblical foundation in their lives.

1 **Knowing Jesus Christ as Lord**
God's purpose for our lives through a personal relationship with Jesus

2 **The New Way of Living**
True repentance and faith toward God

3 **New Testament Baptisms**
Four baptisms including baptism in water and baptism in the Holy Spirit

4 **Building For Eternity**
The hope of the resurrection, the laying on of hands and eternal judgment

5 **Living in the Grace of God**
Applying God's grace to everyday living

6 **Freedom from the Curse**
Christ brings freedom to every area of our lives

7 **Learning to Fellowship with God**
How to deepen our relationship with Jesus Christ

8 **What is the Church?**
Finding our place in God's family

9 **Authority and Accountability**
How to respond to leadership and fellow believers God places in our lives

10 **God's Perspective on Finances**
How God wants His people to handle money

11 **Called to Minister**
Every Christian's call to serve

12 **The Great Commission**
Our purpose for living on this planet

A corresponding *Biblical Foundations for Children* book is also available.

For other House To House Pulications resources:
call 1-800-848-5892
www.dcfi.org   email: dcfi@dcfi.org

Introduction

The foundation of the Christian faith is built on Jesus Christ and His Word to us, the Holy Bible. This twelve-book *Biblical Foundation Series* includes elementary principles every Christian needs to help lay a strong spiritual foundation in his or her life.

In this sixth Biblical Foundation book, *Freedom From the Curse,* we learn that due to Adam and Eve's disobedience to the Lord when they chose to believe the lies of the devil in the Garden of Eden, we now live in a "cursed or fallen" world. In the fall of Adam, sin gained entrance into the human race. In this book, we will take a closer look at all that is involved in the curse and how to be freed spiritually, physically and emotionally from its bondage(s). Although sin has cursed mankind, Christ provides everything we need to defeat sin and Satan!

In this book, the foundation truths from the Word of God are presented with modern day parables that help you easily understand the basics of Christianity. Use this book and the other 11 *Biblical Foundation* books to lay a solid spiritual foundation in your life, or if you are already a mature Christian, these books are great tools to assist you in discipling others. May His Word become life to you today.

God bless you!
Larry Kreider

How to Use This Resource

Personal study

Read from start to finish as an individual study program to build a firm Christian foundation and develop spiritual maturity.

- Each chapter has a key verse excellent to commit to memory.
- Additional scriptures in gray boxes are used for further study.
- Each reading includes questions for personal reflection and room to journal at the end of the book.

Daily devotional

Use as a devotional for a daily study of God's Word.

- Each chapter is divided into 7-day sections for weekly use.
- Additional days at the end of the book bring the total number of devotionals to one complete month. The complete set of 12 books gives one year's worth of daily devotionals.
- Additional scriptures are used for further study.
- Each day includes reflection questions and a place to write answers at the end of the book.

Mentoring relationship

Use for a spiritual parenting relationship to study, pray and discuss life applications together.

- A spiritual father or mother can easily take a spiritual son or daughter through these short Bible study lessons and use the reflection questions to provoke dialogue about what is learned.
- Read each day or an entire chapter at a time.

Small group study

Study this important biblical foundation in a small group setting.

- The teacher studies the material in the chapters and teaches, using the user-friendly outline provided at the end of the book.

Taught as a biblical foundation course

These teachings can be taught by a pastor or other Christian leader as a basic biblical foundation course.

- Students read an assigned portion of the material.
- In the class, the leader teaches the assigned material using the chapter outlines at the end of the book.

CHAPTER 1

What is a Curse?

KEY MEMORY VERSE

Christ redeemed us from the curse of the law by
becoming a curse for us, for it is written:
"Cursed is everyone who is hung on a tree."
Galatians 3:13

Sin enters a perfect world and changes it forever

God had a perfect plan for this world. His plan for the human race, starting with Adam and Eve, was that all of creation would be blessed. There would be no sickness, disease or poverty. There would be only beauty and health and abundance. However, Adam and Eve disobeyed the commandment God gave them about the tree of the knowledge of good and evil, and sin entered the world. They trusted in themselves and in their own ability to make a decision that seemed right in their eyes instead of obeying God, and they made a fatal mistake. This mistake has affected all of us. *Therefore, just as sin entered the world through one man, and death through sin, and in this way death came to all men, because all sinned (Romans 5:12).*

> **We are born with an impulse toward sin**
> Romans 5:19; 1:21;7:24
> Genesis 6:5,12; 8:21
> Psalms 14:1-3; Jeremiah 17:9
> Mark 7:21-22
> 1 Corinthians 2:14
> Galatians 5:19; Ephesians 2:1-3
> Colossians 1:21; 1 John 5:19

Due to Adam and Eve's disobedience to the Lord when they chose to believe the lies of the devil, we now live in a "cursed or fallen" world. In the fall of Adam, sin gained entrance into the human race. All humans are now born into the world with an impulse toward sin and evil. Each of us comes into the world with a sinful nature and has the natural tendency to go our own selfish way with little concern for God or others (Romans 8:5-8).

REFLECTION
How did sin curse this world (Romans 5:12)? What does our sinful nature cause us to do?

Satan now causes havoc in the world

Because of what Adam and Eve did by breaking the law God gave them, the ground (nature) was cursed. God told Adam, *...cursed is the ground because of you; through painful toil you will eat of it all the days of your life (Genesis 3:17b).* Adam would now have to work with sweat and toil in order to provide for himself, and eventually death would come to him and his offspring.

Sin and its curse began to increase in the world, and the world experienced the "wages" of this sin. *The wages which sin pays is death (Romans 6:23 Amplified).* This "death" includes all the heartaches and miseries that come from sin. Sin brings destruction into every area of our human existence.

We can see sin's destruction evidenced in the misery people experience in today's world—hundreds die from AIDS every week, and hundreds more are infected by this killer virus...a relative or friend may suddenly have a heart attack...another may die of cancer...brutal gang rapes, murder, violence...there seems to be an upsurge of atrocious crimes being committed daily. Who is responsible for these horrors? If God really cares, some people ask, why are people starving in parts of the world? I believe it all boils down to the fact that we are constantly faced with the power and activity of Satan in this world in one way or another. From the beginning of time, he has caused havoc in the world. Satan intends to afflict us with his lies and treachery. Down through the ages, Satan and his demons have continued to plague mankind as a result of the initial curse.

> **God provides what we need to defeat sin and Satan**
> 1 John 4:4; 5:4-5; Revelation 3:21
> Romans 6:1-14; Colossians 2:6-15
> Hebrews 2:14-15; Ephesians 6:10

In this book, we will take a closer look at all that is involved in the curse and how to be freed from its bondage(s). Although sin has cursed mankind, praise God, Christ provided everything we need to defeat sin and Satan!

REFLECTION
Why was the ground cursed in Genesis 3:17? What happened as a result (Romans 6:23)?

Jesus reigns over the devil

Satan is the father of sin and the god of this world system. He brought sin into the world and tries to entice people to all sorts of evil. He controls this present evil age because the world is in rebellion against God's rule and enslaved to Satan (2 Corinthians 4:4; Luke 13:16; Galatians 1:4; Ephesians 6:12; Hebrews 2:14). But the glorious, good news is that Jesus came to destroy the works of the devil! He came to dissolve the power, influence and connection of sin in our lives. The Bible tells us in 1 John 3:8 that ...*the reason the Son of God appeared was to destroy the devil's work.*

Jesus has undertaken a holy war against Satan who wants to ruin the work of God in this world. This was Jesus' purpose for coming to the earth two thousand years ago. Jesus' plan is to destroy the works of the devil in our lives! He came to establish God's kingdom in our hearts and deliver us from Satan's dominion. By his death and resurrection, Christ initiated the defeat of Satan which will eventually culminate in complete and total victory over Satan at the end of this age. Because of Jesus, we do not have to fear the curse and its effects. Jesus is more powerful than Satan! Jesus acknowledges His supreme power over the devil, the ruler of this world, in John 14:30 when He says...*the prince of this world is coming. He has no hold on me.*

Jesus also says, *You, dear children, are from God and have overcome them, because the one who is in you is greater than the one who is in the world (1 John 4:4).*

REFLECTION
*Why did Jesus come,
according to 1 John 3:8?
How does Jesus destroy the
works of the devil in our lives?*

The Holy Spirit, who lives in every Christian, is greater and more powerful than the devil and his demons who are in the world. He will fight our battles and give us the victory. We can overcome the devil and his evil schemes in this world because we have been given the victory through Jesus!

Jesus became a curse for us

DAY 4

We can be completely free from the curse of breaking God's law. We can be free from the devil's lies over our lives because of what Christ did on the cross. The Bible says He redeemed us from the curse. *Christ redeemed us from the curse of the law by becoming a curse for us, for it is written: "Cursed is everyone who is hung on a tree" (Galatians 3:13).*

When the mob called for Jesus to be crucified, they wanted Him identified as a cursed person because according to Jewish law, anyone who hung on a tree was under God's curse (Deuteronomy 21:23). So Jesus, in our behalf, was crucified and became a curse for us. He was crowned with a crown of thorns, the very symbol of sin and guilt, because he is the Lamb of God that takes away the sin of the world! Every curse over our lives was placed on Jesus when He hung on the cross nearly two thousand years ago! We are redeemed and set free of the curse!

The word _redeemed_ means _to buy back_. I've heard the story of a young boy, who after spending many hours constructing a little boat, took it out on the lake to sail it. With a long string attached to the boat, the boy was having a great time as the boat floated and bobbed. Suddenly, the string tore. In an instant, he lost his prized possession and could only watch as the boat headed downstream where it eventually exited into the river. He thought it was gone forever.

Several years later, this lad entered a pawn shop in a town downstream from where he grew up. He spotted the boat that he had built years before. The young man approached the storekeeper and said, "This is my boat. My initials are carved on the bottom."

The owner said, "Well, I'm sorry, but somebody brought that boat into my store and I bought it from him. You'll need to pay me for it." The young man immediately paid the shopkeeper so he could buy back his cherished boat.

This is a picture of what God did for us. First of all, God made you and me. We went our own way, He redeemed us and bought us back again. By the blood that Jesus shed on the cross two thousand years ago, we have been redeemed (or bought back) from the curse of breaking God's law (sin) that was over our lives.

REFLECTION
How can we be free of the curse of the law (Galatians 3:13)? What does it mean to be redeemed? ➤ _To be bought back._

Jesus broke the curse, but we must seek the freedom. The devil can keep the curse over people's lives when they do not know that Jesus has given them authority to break the curse or when they do not walk in the authority of Christ who sets them free.

People suffer because our planet was turned over to the powers of darkness

If we have been redeemed and set free, why then, along with the rest of mankind, do Christians suffer financial loss, serious illness, emotional upheaval and other problems? The reason people suffer varies greatly. In this section, we are going to take a look at the first of three general reasons why people suffer in this world.

Jesus once healed a man who was blind from birth (John 9:1-3). The disciples asked Jesus, "Who sinned, this man or his parents, that he was born blind?" Jesus answered that neither the man nor his parents had sinned. Why had he suffered then? It was through no fault of his own that he was born blind. Why do people often find themselves afflicted in some way or another with no apparent fault of their own?

We have to go back to the fact that there is a curse in the world. We learned earlier that sin entered the world through the "curse of the law." The curse of the law is God's label for all the distresses experienced as a result of mankind's initial sin. Since the time that Adam and Eve disobeyed God (broke His law or sinned), *we live on a planet that was turned over to the powers of darkness.* Ever since that time, the world has suffered under Satan's rule. Believers along with nonbelievers experience suffering as an ongoing consequence of the fall of Adam and Eve. Much of what happens often is simply the result of life in a fallen world. For example, cancer and other diseases may be the result of an unhealthy diet of highly processed foods, foods that have lost their food value due to pesticides, preservatives and chemicals.

Imagine this scenario. A beautiful garden is given to an evil landlord. What was once filled with beautiful flowers, plants, and food, is soon filled with thistles and thorns. One day a kind and caring man pays a great price and purchases the garden. He gives it back to the former caretakers and gives them clear instructions to make it beautiful and profitable again. Bit by bit, with much hard work, the garden becomes alive. This is what Jesus did for mankind! He paid the great price of His own life in order to purchase back the world. Jesus went to the cross to initiate the defeat of Satan and destroy Satan's power in our lives. We have been given the authority as followers of Jesus on this earth, to replace evil with love, health, forgiveness, peace and blessing for all.

God never intended for wars, disease, cancer, murder, starvation, and poverty to be a part of His plan. God does not cause the evil that happens to us in this world (James 1:13). However, God is sovereign and allows the evil in the world to happen under His permissive will. At times He will directly intervene, but often He allows bad to happen even though He does not desire it. Evil often continues unabated in this world because the devil continues to operate through individuals that do not serve God and have no power over the devil to resist evil.

God permits evil to continue for the time being. But at the end of the age, Satan will experience His final demise when God throws him into the lake of fire forever (Revelation 20:7-10).

Until that time, says Romans 8:23, believers groan inwardly, because of the effects of living in a sinful world. *We ourselves, who have the firstfruits of the Spirit, groan inwardly as we wait eagerly for our adoption as sons, the redemption of our bodies.*

Although we have the Spirit and His blessings, we still groan inwardly because we live in a sinful world and experience its imperfections, pain and sorrow. We are groaning for the complete redemption that will be given at the resurrection when the glory of God will be revealed (2 Corinthians 5:4). Until that time, we must walk in God's grace, strength and comfort which brings spiritual victory in our lives.

REFLECTION
In light of the suffering caused by Satan on this earth, what is our responsibility as Christians?

People suffer because humans make wrong choices

A second reason why people (both believers and unbelievers) suffer on our planet is simply this: *People make wrong choices.* God created mankind to have fellowship with Him. He did not create robots who were programmed to make perfect choices. God wants us to fellowship with Him and obey Him because we want to, not because we have to. God made us in His image with the ability to choose. And sometimes our choices are bad. What happens then?

There is a law in this universe set up by God called "the law of sowing and reaping." The Bible says in Galatians 6:7 that...*a man reaps what he sows.* In other words, if we make wrong choices in life, we will have to reap the consequences. If we drive recklessly, we will probably have an accident. If we mistreat our bodies, we may have serious health problems. If we refuse to work, we may have to go without food and clothing. The sin of immorality and adultery often results in the breakdown of a marriage.

Wrong choices not only affect an individual, it may affect his family and those around him and even future generations. An alcoholic father not only ruins his own life but his life-style has a devastating effect on his whole family. The Bible says that the sins of parents can follow their children to the third and fourth generations (Exodus 20:5; Deuteronomy 5:9).

A young man I was counseling once told me he didn't want to end up like his father. His father's life-style and example was deplorable and undesirable. Sometime later, this man chose to turn away from Christ, and the most astonishing thing happened during the next few years. The young man's life-style and characteristics became like those of his father. Since this young man was no longer living in obedience to Jesus Christ as his Lord, he was unable to break the curse that was passed down from his father's generation to his generation. In fact, this curse had been passed down to his life from many preceding generations and caused him to continue to live in bondage. This is why Jesus gave His life on the cross. He became a curse for us so that we no longer need to fear reaping what was sown by our ancestors. (For more on breaking generational curses or strongholds, see Chapter 4, Day 6.)

As Christians, we must act in accord with God's Word and avoid whatever will remove us from God's protection. We must confess known sin and examine our lives to see if we are displeasing the Holy Spirit. However, when we do make bad choices, even innocently, God may allow hardships and suffering in our lives as a means of discipline so we again submit to His will and walk in faith. When God disciplines us, He does so because He loves us, according to Hebrews 12:5-6. *My son, do not make light of the Lord's discipline, and do not lose heart when he rebukes you, because the Lord disciplines those he loves, and he punishes everyone he accepts as a son.*

God wants us to live holy lives as His children. Suffering is sometimes a tool God uses to get our attention. He wants to accomplish His purposes for our lives and get us to trust Him completely. Sometimes we must endure hardships because they can serve as a catalyst to spiritual growth. *No discipline seems pleasant at the time, but painful. Later on, however, it produces a harvest of righteousness and peace for those who have*

REFLECTION

How do our choices make a difference in the way our lives are lived?

Is it possible to be affected by the sins of our ancestors?

yes.

been trained by it (Hebrews 12:11). Suffering forces us to trust in God rather than ourselves.

People suffer because of direct satanic attack

Direct satanic attack is a third reason people suffer in this world. The New Testament is filled with people who suffered because demons tormented them, and it continues to happen today.

Demonic curses are sometimes placed on a person so that he or she is crippled emotionally, spiritually, and even physically. The word *curse* means *to call evil down, or to bring evil on, or to afflict.* Those involved in satanic cults sometimes attempt to place curses on others. People who have had curses placed on them may have an unexplained accident or go through specific kinds of problems.

Balak, king of the Moabites, tried to place a curse on the Israelites who were coming in his direction. Balak had heard the stories of how the God of the Israelites had destroyed their enemies, and he was scared. So he called a prophet named Balaam and asked him to put a curse on the people of Israel. His plan did not work. The children of Israel had chosen to follow God's plan for their lives, and no enemy could defeat them (Numbers 22).

Believers are not always immune to Satan's attacks and bondages. Even though Job was a righteous man who walked with God, the Lord allowed Satan to attack him. Paul was a spirit-filled godly man, yet he experienced a "thorn in the flesh" that he described as a messenger of Satan. Both men suffered, but God used their afflictions to teach them important spiritual lessons. These men learned to live victoriously because they knew they ultimately had authority over the power of Satan and his demons just as we do today.

Usually direct satanic attack occurs for two reasons:

1. We are not walking under the protection of Christ or fail to walk in His power, therefore opening our lives up to demonic attack.

2. In the case of Paul, he was walking in such a great revelation that Jesus allowed Satan access to him so he would not become proud (2 Corinthians 12:7).

We must break the power of Satan by waging intense spiritual warfare. We live in a spirit world. The enemy is out to destroy us any way he can. The devil has come to steal, kill and destroy (John 10:10). When Satan can attack, he will. As Christians we must be alert to Satan's schemes. *Be self-controlled and alert. Your enemy the devil prowls around like a roaring lion looking for someone to devour. Resist him, standing firm in the faith, because you know that your brothers throughout the world are undergoing the same kind of sufferings. And the God of all grace, who called you to his eternal glory in Christ, after you have suffered a little while, will himself restore you and make you strong, firm and steadfast (1 Peter 5:8-10).*

Although, as Christians, we do not have to walk in fear of Satan and his demons, Satan is our enemy. We have been delivered from his power, but as a roaring lion, he remains a threat to us and seeks to destroy us. We must stand firm in the faith. No matter what kind of suffering he inflicts, or how he tries to influence our emotions, our thoughts or our actions, God will see us through.

REFLECTION

Are believers immune to Satan's attacks? No

How can we be alert to Satan's schemes (1 Peter 5:8-10)? Resist, Remember brothers + endure

We Can Reclaim What the Enemy Stole

We can be victorious!

If we have the power of God living in us and are set free from the curse of the law, then why are some Christians living as if they have not been redeemed and set free? Yes, even Christians may find themselves in areas of bondages. Even though we have given our lives to Jesus Christ and are filled with His Holy Spirit, there may be areas of bondage in our lives we continue to deal with.

First of all, as Christians, we need to realize that **we can have victory in every area of our lives!** This victory is promised in the first book of the Bible when God promises to redeem the world, giving us the victory over Satan.

The devil is the most cursed being in the entire universe, and his demise is certain. That's why he wars so relentlessly against God and His people. But his fate was already sealed in the third chapter of Genesis. God tells the serpent that there would be a spiritual conflict between the offspring of the woman (Jesus Christ) and the offspring of the serpent (Satan and his demons). *So the Lord God said to the serpent, "Because you have done this, cursed are you above all the livestock and all the wild animals! You will crawl on your belly and you will eat dust all the days of your life. And I will put enmity between you and the woman, and between your offspring and hers; he will crush your head, and you will strike his heel"* (Genesis 3:14-15).

God promises that Christ would be born of a woman and be "struck" through His crucifixion. But even though He was struck, He would rise from the dead to completely crush Satan, sin and death. Jesus came to earth to deliver us from Satan's dominion and establish God's kingdom in our hearts. He came to give us life and victory!

Tragedies are not a part of God's plan for your life—they have not originated in heaven. The Bible tells us clearly that every good gift comes from above (James 1:17). One of Satan's most subtle schemes is to try to cause us to blame God for the bad things that happen in our lives. We have already discussed that the trials and sufferings in our lives have various causes—because we live in a sinful world, because we make wrong choices or due to direct satanic attack. If we look at the root of all of these causes, notice that they have Satan at their core! So we can never blame God.

God is the One who provides a way out of our bondage to sin and suffering. He has a plan for our lives. It is a plan that is filled with hope. God can take the most negative circumstances and turn them around for good. No matter how dark our circumstances seem at the moment, we can be full of hope. Jesus helps us to come through every obstacle victoriously. His plans for you are plans of peace and not of evil. He wants to give you a future and a hope (Jeremiah 29:11).

Jesus understands suffering, because He was willing to suffer more than anyone ever has, by taking our sins upon Himself when He died on the cross. There, he broke the powers of darkness and provided forgiveness for us, setting us free from the curse.

We live in a covenant relationship with God

DAY 2

We must realize, like Abraham did, that we have a covenant with God. In a covenant made with Abraham in Genesis 17:7, God promised, *I will establish my covenant as an everlasting covenant between me and you and your descendants after you for the generations to come, to be your God...*

With this Old Testament covenant, God promises Abraham to bind Himself to His faithful people to be their God. God continued this relationship in the New Testament where He made a new covenant with us in Jesus Christ. The new covenant is a promise to bestow divine protection and blessing on those who, through faith, accept Christ and receive His promises. Galatians 3:6-9 says, *Consider Abraham: "He believed God, and it was credited to him as righteousness." Understand, then, that those who believe are children of Abraham. The Scripture foresaw that God would justify the Gentiles by faith, and announced the gospel in advance to Abraham: "All nations will be blessed through you." So those who have faith are blessed along with Abraham, the man of faith.*

All who believe, as Abraham believed, share in Abraham's blessings. We have inherited the blessing of Abraham through faith in Jesus Christ. Faith brings blessing.

Our relationship with God is secured by His blood, but the depth of our fellowship with Him may fluctuate. It depends on our obedience to God. We must maintain a close fellowship with God so we can be blessed according to Deuteronomy 28:1-3.

But if we do not heed the voice of the Lord, we will be under a curse (v. 15). A curse is the absence of a blessing. The consequences of turning away from fellowshipping with God results in a curse on our lives. We cannot expect God to bless us if we have turned away from Him.

Nevertheless, believers are assured that if they love Jesus and depend on Him, He will never leave or forsake them. He will be their helper through any difficulties. Jesus Christ has come to set us free, to be whole, in every area of life.

It is not the will of God for evil to come upon our lives. It's not God's will for sickness, confusion, depression, fear, insecurity or inferiority to come upon us. However, as we learned before, we will not always be exempt from suffering. That does not negate the fact that God wants us to be free from all of these afflictions. They are a part of the original curse, and God wants us to be free. He has created us to be whole!

When I was a child, I had a heart murmur. Some of my relatives also had heart problems. I believe it was a product of a curse genetically passed down from generation to generation. When my schoolmates were having fun playing sports, I had to stand on the sidelines and watch. Often, to make matters worse, the teachers recruited me to be the umpire. Every time I had to call a close play, the team that didn't agree with me let me know in no uncertain terms they thought I was a lousy umpire.

REFLECTION *my obe*
What does our covenant with Jesus Christ depend upon? Name some areas that are a part of the original curse. How can we be set free?
temper, lust, weight allow Christ to become a c

But, praise God, today I have been set free and healed of not only those memories but of the heart murmur as well! Today I can play baseball, basketball, and football and for enjoy every minute of it. It is all because Jesus Christ became a curse for me. I am reaping the benefits of my relationship or covenant with Him!

We cannot allow the enemy to lie to us

It is true that Christians get sick and depressed. Christians sometimes struggle with temper tantrums in the same way their parents and grandparents struggled with hot tempers. Even Christians may be susceptible to a curse that has been passed down through the family line, continuing unchecked for generations. The beautiful truth for us to know is that we can be set free from those curses in Jesus' name! We do not have to wallow helplessly in a life-controlling habit, sin or curse.

Because of our disobedience to the Lord before we came to know Jesus, we deserve to experience the curse on our lives. However, because of faith in Jesus and the grace of God, we can rise up and walk in the freedom that comes from knowing Jesus Christ.

The devil has lied to many of us. He is the father of all lies (John 8:44). Probably the devil has lied to you. Maybe he told you that you can't help yourself because the problems that you deal with are the same kind of problems and tendencies that you see in your parents. The truth is this: You may not have been able to help yourself before you received Jesus into your life, but when you were born again, things changed. You have a new Father in heaven. Your new daddy is not under the curse. Your new father in heaven does not have temper tantrums. Your new Father in heaven has not been struggling with cancer or migraine headaches or heart problems or whatever else may have "grown" into your family tree. Your new Father in heaven will set you free from every curse.

Many times people "prophesy" over us in negative ways. Parents tell their children, "You're just like your dad; you have his bad temper." Or, "You'll never amount to anything." We can break these negative "prophesies" in the name of Jesus Christ. They are a part of the curse. God loves you. He cares about you. That is why He went to the cross, so that all of our insecurities and fears and all those curses from past generations can be broken (see Chapter 4, Day 6).

God wants to give you and me good gifts. James 1:17 tells us, *Every good and perfect gift is from above, coming down from the Father of the heavenly lights, who does not change like shifting shadows.*

REFLECTION
Has the devil lied to you about an area of your life in which you do not seem to have victory? Yes, trust *What can you do about it?*
Rise up 'n victory with Jesus.

We must stake our claim!

We know that Jesus came to set us free from every curse the enemy wants to place in our lives. Romans 5:15,19 tells us that Adam brought sin and death, but Christ brought grace and life. *For if the many died by the trespass of the one man [Adam], how much more did God's grace and the gift that came by the grace of the one man, Jesus Christ, overflow to the many! For just as through the disobedience of the one man [Adam] the many were made sinners, so also through the obedience of the one man [Jesus] the many will be made righteous.*

Christ reclaimed what Satan tried to take from us. We need to take back the areas of our lives that our enemy, the devil, has stolen from us.

The children of Israel went into Canaan, the new land that God promised to them. This new land was legally their land. God had told them clearly, "I'll give it to you." However, they had to go in and receive it, step by step. They had to walk in and claim it. Joshua 1:3 says, *I will give you every place where you set your foot, as I promised Moses.*

In other words, God told Joshua, "Joshua, the land is yours, but you have to go in and claim it. You must take it back from your enemies." If the devil has stolen your peace, your joy, your health, or your hope, today is your day to claim it back from the enemy!

The children of Israel went to the city of Jericho, marched around seven times, shouted, and the walls came down. Even though it was theirs for the taking, they had to physically go in and claim it. You may say, "Well, I'm a Christian. Doesn't this all happen automatically?" Legally, yes, it's yours. But practically, in order to experience it, you need to go in and claim back from the devil the specific areas that he has stolen from you.

REFLECTION
What does the Lord promise to those who want to reclaim what Satan has taken from them (Joshua 1:3)? He will redeem all this + reclaim it for us.

We apply God's Word to our lives

Christians have been delivered from the power of darkness and are now in Christ's kingdom (Colossians 1:13). It is faith that unlocks the door. It is faith that makes the difference in our lives. Joshua was a man of faith. That's why he marched around the city of Jericho for seven days. As a man of faith, he obeyed God's Word and claimed the inheritance that the Lord had promised him. When we believe what God says in His Word, we will find ourselves being freed from depression, inferiority, insecurities, fears of mental illness, sickness and disease. It is faith that unlocks the door. Romans 5:17 tells us clearly, *For if, by the trespass of the one man, death reigned through that one man, how much more will those who receive God's abundant provision of grace and of the gift of righteousness reign in life through the one man, Jesus Christ.*

God has called us to reign in life, to live a victorious life in Christ. If I give you a gift certificate for one thousand dollars, that gift certificate is worthless until you cash it in. The same is true of the Word of God. In order to walk victoriously in our spiritual lives, we have to seek, learn and grow in the knowledge of God through His Word. We cannot grow without God's Word and we cannot change without it. God's Word motivates us to obedience and fellowship with Him. We need to take the Word of God and begin to apply it to every area of our lives so that we can experience the wholeness that God has promised. By doing so, we reclaim what the devil has tried to steal from us. God's Word is an indispensable weapon in Christian warfare against the devil. *Take the...sword of the Spirit, which is the word of God (Ephesians 6:17).*

In Ephesians 6, we see there are other items of Christian armor—the belt, the breastplate, the shoes, the shield and the helmet—all intended for defense. The Word of God is the only weapon of attack. We must know God's Word and apply it to our lives so we can attack the powers of darkness in our lives and put them to flight.

This may or may not happen overnight. God is a God of miracles and may move supernaturally and quickly to alter or heal a problem in our lives. But many times, He changes us through a more gradual process of growth and change. It takes more faith and character to persevere through problems, and God wants us to use His Word to overcome in this way.

To overcome life-dominating patterns in our lives or any other trial or temptation that confronts us, we need to be honest with God and confess our weakness and dependency on Him. As we confess the truth of God's Word, faith is built in our hearts (Romans 10:17). And as faith is built, we begin to experience the Lord's wholeness.

For example, if we struggle with depression, we should pray, *Father in Jesus' name, this depression and despondency has no hold on me. I am set free by the blood of Jesus and the power of His Spirit. Soul, be encouraged in Jesus' name!*

REFLECTION Sword of the sp God's Word is likened to what offensive weapon (Ephesians 6:17)? How can we attack the powers of darkness and put them to flight (Romans 10:17)?

Confess the sin, claim the victory, & the truth.

We guard our tongues

We must be careful how we speak. Matthew 12:34 says, *For out of the abundance of the heart the mouth speaks.* In other words, we believe with the heart, and what we speak is often what we really believe. The Bible also says we will be judged by our words. *But I tell you that men will have to give account on the day of judgment for every careless word they have spoken. For by your words you will be acquitted, and by your words you will be condemned (Matthew 12:36-37).* Life and death are in the power of the tongue.

By our speech, we can pronounce either a blessing or a curse. If we continually say, "I think I'm going to get sick," we can begin to pronounce a curse of sickness on our lives. Instead we need to say, "I feel like I'm getting sick, but I know that God desires for me to be a whole person, and I can receive His healing." By speaking words of faith, we pronounce a blessing on our lives.

Sometimes people say, "My mother had a miscarriage, maybe I'll have a miscarriage too." By believing these words, we can begin to open the door for the devil to lay what we speak on our lives. The enemy will attempt to use these words to place fear in our lives, and the things that we fear can come upon us. Job 3:25 tells us, *For the thing I greatly feared has come upon me, And what I dreaded has happened to me.* Fear is destroyed as we speak the Word of God to ourselves and to others around us. God tells us in 2 Timothy 1:7, *For God has not given us a spirit of fear, but of power and of love and of a sound mind.*

You may ask, "Why does it matter what we say, as long as our hearts are right?" Imagine walking into a bank with a toy water pistol and saying, "I'll take ten thousand dollars, please." The teller, seeing the gun, activates the alarm. The police rush in and arrest you. "I'm only kidding," you say. "It's only a water pistol. I was just joking. I didn't really mean it." Maybe you did not mean it, but you will end up in jail for the words you said and the action you took! The same principle applies to spiritual things. The devil is a legalist. He will use our words against us. We

REFLECTION
How can the words you say condemn you? Give examples from your life. I'll be damned,

need to be careful how we speak. We need to speak the things that God says in His Word. We need to speak life-giving words that release hope in people's lives.

We release our inheritance

Our God promises us wholeness and health and victory in every area of our lives. *If you belong to Christ, then you are Abraham's seed, and heirs according to the promise (Galatians 3:29).*

The Spirit himself testifies with our spirit that we are God's children (Romans 8:16).

We are God's children through faith in Jesus Christ! God speaks to us by the Holy Spirit and tells us we are heirs of His promises. He is the God who said He would bless Abraham, and by faith you and I are also the children of Abraham. You may ask, "If I am really an heir of God, then why do I still deal with depression?" We must remember, the New Testament is the new covenant or will that our Father in heaven has left for us. If your uncle dies, and wills you his inheritance, you must sign the proper documents to release the inheritance before you can receive it. Spiritually, we must receive our inheritance from God in order to be set free.

We are free from the curse when we realize what the Word of God, the Lord's will and our inheritance says, and we act on it. For example, if you are feeling weak today, claim the strength the Lord promises in His Word. The Bible says, *I can do everything through him who gives me strength (Philippians 4:13).* Confess this promise and receive His strength today!

I was driving down the road in my car one day when a spirit of fear came on me like a cloud. I was paralyzed with fear. Immediately I was aware of what was happening. The enemy was trying to cause me to live by my feelings of fear rather than doing the things I knew God was calling me to do. I said boldly, "In Jesus' name, I renounce this spirit of fear and command it to leave." And guess what? It left! When we resist the devil, he has to flee! (James 4:7).

A few years ago, I was in Europe and experienced a similar spirit of fear. Again, this spirit of fear had to leave when confronted with the name of Jesus. Jesus Christ became a curse for us. We do not have to put up with a spirit of fear or any other affliction that the devil will try to bring against us. Jesus Christ has come to set us free!

REFLECTION

*When we realize what our inheritance is, how do we release it?
Speak Philippians 4:13 aloud.*

* When we act upon the promises & word of God.

Receiving Freedom in Jesus' Name

Free spiritually!

In these next two chapters, we will look at seven areas of freedom that we can experience as believers in Jesus Christ. First of all, let's take a look at *spiritual freedom.* 1 John 1:9 says, *If we confess our sins, he is faithful and just and will forgive us our sins and purify us from all unrighteousness.*

After we have given our lives to Jesus, the devil may try to paralyze us spiritually by telling us that we are not really saved. He is a liar! The Bible tells us in Romans 8:1-2, *Therefore, there is now no condemnation for those who are in Christ Jesus, because through Christ Jesus the law of the Spirit of life set me free from the law of sin and death.* There is no condemnation to those who are in Christ. And remember, there is a big difference between God's conviction and the enemy's condemnation. God's conviction always brings hope. But the devil's condemnation brings hopelessness.

The Bible tells us, *For God is not a God of disorder but of peace...(1 Corinthians 14:33).* If your heart is turned toward the Lord and you are still experiencing spiritual doubts and confusion in your life, it is not from God. The devil is the author of confusion and condemnation. Jesus paid the price for this curse to be broken.

I dealt with times of intense guilt after I gave my life to Jesus. One day, I got tired of it. I opened my Bible to 1 John 1:9, and declared to the devil, "I'm believing the Word of God, instead of what I feel in my emotions." Do you know what happened? I was set free. I later realized that the enemy had placed a curse over me. That curse of false guilt was trying to push me into depression, confusion and frustration, but it was broken that night in Jesus' name.

REFLECTION
How do you get rid of feelings of guilt and condemnation (Romans 8:1-2)? What is the difference between conviction and condemnation?

I am reminded of the story of a farmer who was battling with false guilt and confusion in his life. He wasn't sure he was saved. Finally, he went to the back of his barn, took a big stake and hammered it into the ground. He confessed, "Jesus, you are the Lord of my life." He believed in his heart that Jesus was alive from the dead (Romans 10:9). Then He made a bold statement. "It happened right here at this stake. I gave my life completely to God. The next

* You choose to believe God's word + not a human emotion
28   also you look at the fruit of it. Is this general
the healthy response God would say yeah + amen he?
+ Condemnation brings with it the fruit of death

time the devil lies to me, I'm going right back here to this stake as proof. From this moment on, I will know, that I know, I am saved!" How could he know? Because he knew the curse of false guilt and confusion was broken because of Jesus Christ. He had made a decision to believe the truth, the Word of God. His life was different from that day on.

Free from sickness and disease

A second area of freedom has to do with *freedom from sickness and disease*. Physical healing is sometimes controversial in the body of Christ. Let's see what the Bible has to say. Matthew 8:16-17 tells us, *When evening came, many who were demon-possessed were brought to him, and he drove out the spirits with a word and healed all the sick. This was to fulfill what was spoken through the prophet Isaiah: "He took up our infirmities and carried our diseases."*

According to the new covenant, the New Testament, it is God's will that you and I are healed and healthy. When Jesus Christ went to the cross two thousand years ago, He provided forgiveness for sin, eternal and resurrection life for death, and *healing for sickness!* Freedom from the curse also includes the area of physical healing.

Jesus healed people who came to Him for healing. Matthew, chapter eight, tells us that when the people came to Him, He healed them. He was fulfilling the prophecy in the Old Testament from the book of Isaiah 53:4-5 that says, *Surely he took up our infirmities...and by his wounds we are healed.* 1 Peter 2:24 says it similarly: *He himself bore our sins in his body on the tree, so that we might die to sins and live for righteousness; by his wounds you have been healed.*

While Jesus was teaching in a synagogue one Sabbath, He called a woman forward who was crippled by a spirit of infirmity which was a direct result of demonic activity. We should note here that although Jesus healed many diseases, not all of them were attributed to demonic causes. However, in this case it was. Jesus laid His hands on her and immediately she was made straight, and glorified God (Luke 13:13). The ruler of the synagogue was indignant. He was not accustomed to this kind of thing happening in his religious meetings. Sometimes religious people have problems believing that we can be free from the curse of sickness and disease. Nevertheless, it could not be denied, Jesus Christ set the

Conviction brings without change, repentance + the fruit of life.

woman free. The same can happen today. The Bible tells us, Jesus Christ is the same yesterday, today, and forever (Hebrews 13:8).

Every sickness, every type of cancer, every case of heart failure, every migraine headache has been hung on the cross through Jesus Christ. We need to take God's Word seriously and place our faith in the Word of God instead of on the symptoms we see in our body. We must seek the presence of Jesus in our lives and saturate our lives with God's Word. We should expect a miracle (Matthew 7:8; 19:26).

I mentioned earlier in this book that I had a heart murmur as a young man. But a short time after coming to know Jesus Christ as Lord, my doctor found I had been made completely whole. By the grace of God, I am completely free from any heart murmur today.

REFLECTION

Put your name in place of the words "our" and "we" in 1 Peter 2:24. Do you believe God wants you to be free of every sickness and disease?
6h Yes!.

Jesus Christ is our healer because He is the same yesterday, today, and forever.

Hindrances to healing

Sometimes people say, "I know Jesus heals spiritually, but I'm not sure that He heals physically." The truth is that God wants to bless us with both.

Sometime back, a friend who owns a restaurant decided to treat our family to a meal. He told us we could have anything we wanted on the menu, absolutely free. I had a choice to make. I did not deserve this free meal, yet, I was told I could not pay for it. As I looked at all of the sumptuous food I could think, "I don't want to ask for too much. I don't want to take advantage of my friend." My friend would have been disappointed if I had responded that way, and it would have been pride keeping me from receiving a blessing. I believe the Lord responds to us the same way. God's only Son, Jesus Christ, went to the cross so that you and I could take advantage of the precious gift of wholeness that He has given to us. The entire bill has been paid!

Jesus Christ came to set you and me free from every curse including the curse of sickness, disease and all types of physical infirmities in our bodies. I have a friend who was miraculously healed of rheumatic fever. His parents decided to trust the Word of God to see their son healed, and although he was very sick, they chose to believe the Word of God instead of the symptoms they saw. And he was healed! Jesus Christ came to set my friend free from the curse. The Bible says, *Praise the Lord, O my soul, and forget not all his benefits—who forgives all your sins and heals all your diseases (Psalms 103:2-3).*

God wants to heal all our diseases, but sometimes there are hindrances to receiving divine healing, such as, unconfessed sin (James 5:16), demonic oppression or bondage (Luke 13:11-13), fear or acute anxiety (Proverbs 3:5-8; Philippians 4:6-7), past disappointments that undermine present faith (Mark 5:26; John 5:5-7), unbiblical teaching (Mark 3:1-5; 7:13), failure of the leaders to pray the prayer of faith (Mark 11:22-24; James 5:14-16), failure of the church to seek and obtain the gifts of miracles and healings as God intended (Acts 4:29-30; 6:8; 8:5-6; 1 Corinthians 12:9-10,29-31; Hebrews 2:3-4), unbelief (Mark 6:3-6; 9:19,23-24), or self-centered behavior (1 Corinthians 11:29-30). At other times, the reason for the persistence of physical affliction in godly people is not readily apparent (Galatians 4:13; 1 Timothy 5:23; 2 Timothy 4:20). In still other instances, God chooses to take His beloved saints to heaven during an illness (2 Kings 13:14).[1]

If our prayers are not answered for healing, we cannot give up. We should rejoice if healing comes immediately and rejoice if it does not come (Philippians 4:4). God promises to never forsake us or forget us. Sometimes God's purposes for us are for our greater good that we cannot understand.

If we believe the Lord wants us to go to a doctor, then, by all means, we should go to a doctor. But let's go to our Great Physician first! The power of medical science is limited, but the power of God and His Word is unlimited! In the end, it is always Jesus, our Great Physician, who ultimately heals, anyway.

We are learning to live out the promises of God's Word in our Christian lives. We are learning to apply the promises of the Lord's inheritance to our lives. So we must chose to live by what God says in His Word even though we may not see the expected results. Sometimes God tests our hearts to see if we really fear Him. He tested Abraham when He asked him to sacrifice Isaac. Job was tested, too, but in the end he prospered (Job 42:10). God wants to set us free, but He also wants to know that we love Him more than any covenant blessing.

God is getting His church to a place where we will walk together in wholeness and victory as we continue to grow in applying the Word of God to our lives. There are times when we need to do something specific like calling for the elders of our church to pray for us and anoint us with oil. *Is any one of you sick? He should call the elders of the church to pray over him and anoint him with oil in the name of the Lord. And the prayer offered in faith will make the sick person well; the Lord will raise him up...(James 5:14-15).* The Bible tells us if we obey this scrip-

tural mandate, the Lord will "raise us up," heal us and make us completely whole by their prayer of faith.

[1]Full Life Study Bible, (Grand Rapids, Michigan: Zondervan Publishing House, 1992), p. 1421.

Free from painful memories

Many Christians long for a deeper and closer relationship with the Lord. But they continue to struggle with the same fears and hurtful memories from their past, unable to break free. Crippled emotionally, they need to be set free from the curse of painful memories and hurts in their lives. It is not God's will for people's hearts to be broken. He wants to heal us emotionally according to Luke 4:18-19. *The Spirit of the Lord is on me, because he has anointed me to preach good news to the poor. He has sent me to proclaim freedom for the prisoners and recovery of sight for the blind, **to release the oppressed**, to proclaim the year of the Lord's favor.*

A young man and his fiancee came to me for premarital counseling. The young man had experienced many hurts in his life. For one, his father had constantly blamed him for the problems in his marriage because the son was conceived out of wedlock. The young man was hurting and needed healing. I asked him if he was willing to forgive his dad. He was willing. We laid hands on him and prayed for him to be healed of the painful memories he received while growing up.

* pride, false humility - or maybe questioning my own ability of stewardship.

Biblical Foundations

* rejoice the same as if they were !!

The young man had a wonderful wedding a few months later. His father was at his wedding, and there was no longer a wall between them. God had healed him. The pain was gone. God supernaturally healed him because Jesus Christ took that pain on the cross two thousand years ago. Jesus Christ became a curse for that young man.

Sometimes the term, "inner healing" is used for explaining emotional healing. To receive inner healing means to be healed of lie-filled memories or to have our broken hearts healed. Sometimes our present emotional pain comes from the misinterpretations (lies) embedded in our memories and not from the memories themselves. For example, an incest victim feels shame not because she was molested but because she may believe it was her fault (lie). When the lie is exposed, she can receive freedom!

Inner healing, or the healing of memories, is a very valid ministry in the body of Christ today. If we believe someone has hurt us and continue to remember those hurts and the memories of what has happened, we need to be healed emotionally. We can be made whole! Jesus wants to heal us and set us free in His name.

REFLECTION
Do you have painful memories of past hurts? Why do you think you are unable to break free?

The healing of memories does not mean that we no longer remember what has happened. We may remember what happened, but the pain has been healed through Jesus revealing the truth to us. We can look back and now give praise to God for His healing on our lives and His grace and strength to go on.

Forgive, forgive, forgive

We find an important scriptural key to being healed and set free in Matthew 6:14-15. *For if you forgive men when they sin against you, your heavenly Father will also forgive you. But if you do not forgive men their sins, your Father will not forgive your sins.*

This is important! **We must forgive those who have hurt us in order for God to heal us.** In Matthew 18, Jesus tells a parable about a servant who owed his king one million dollars. He begged the king for extra time to pay the debt, and the king had pity on him and canceled the whole debt. The servant then went out and found one of his fellow servants who owed him two thousand dollars. He

Yes, but some memories are just good deterrents & others God has healed me of the affliction, but allows me keep some pain so that my testimony never loses it's sympathetic understanding.

grabbed him by the shirt and demanded immediate payment. The fellow servant pleaded for more time, but the servant refused and had him thrown into prison. The king discovered what had happened and called the servant in. "I forgave you a million dollars and you couldn't forgive someone a few thousand dollars? I showed you mercy but you could not show mercy to another?" Then the scripture makes an interesting statement, *In anger his master turned him over to the jailers to be tortured, until he should pay back all he owed. This is how my heavenly Father will treat each of you unless you forgive your brother from your heart (Matthew 18:34-35).*

The king had the man thrown into prison for not showing forgiveness to another. Jesus says that if we don't forgive someone who has hurt us or "ripped us off," God will deliver us to the *torturers* or *demons of hell.* Even Christians at times can be tor-

REFLECTION

What is the first step in receiving healing of memories (Matthew 6:14-15)?
What happens if we do not forgive (Matthew 18:34-35)?

mented with confusion, frustration, depression, etc. brought on by the demons of hell if they choose not to forgive. Unforgiveness leaves the door wide open for the devil!

Forgiving those who have hurt us is the first step to being set free. We may not feel like it, but because God forgave us, we need to forgive others in Jesus' name. God will bring emotional healing into our lives as we obey His Word and forgive in faith from our hearts.

And forgive some more!

In addition to "forgiving the person who has hurt us," we must also "ask God to forgive the person." Asking God to forgive them, is a vital second step of forgiveness we need to take so that we can be set free. Stephen, when he was being stoned, said, "Father, forgive them." Jesus, on the cross, said, "Father, forgive them, they don't know what they do."

A third step is to "ask God to forgive us for any wrong attitudes or attempt to hide our sin." Proverbs 28:13 says, *He who conceals his sins does not prosper, but whoever confesses and renounces them finds mercy.* The word *prosper* means *to break out of bondage.* If we hide our sin and are not honest about it, we cannot break out

DAY 6

✗ forgiveness
✗ We are bound by our unforgiveness
matt 18

of the bondage in our lives. If we don't ask God to heal us for wrong attitudes, then we cannot prosper in this area of our lives.

A forth step is to "confess our faults to someone" and have him or her pray for us so that God will heal us. The scripture says in James 5:16, *Therefore confess your sins to each other and pray for each other so that you may be healed. The prayer of a righteous man is powerful and effective.*

Ask someone to lay hands on you and pray for emotional healing. This is why it is so important to be connected to the rest of the body of Christ through a local church. As you meet together with other believers, ask the Lord to show you someone whom you can trust to pray for you. The Lord wants to heal you and set you free from the curse in Jesus' name.

Corrie ten Boom, who experienced life in a Nazi concentration camp and whose life story inspired the movie, "The Hiding Place," often spoke about "the ding-dong theory." A church bell rings ding-dong, ding-dong, ding-dong after someone pulls the long chord attached to the ringer. The ding-dong begins very loud and then grows softer and softer until it finally stops ringing. Corrie said that when you ask the Lord to heal you, the devil may try to bring some of those old emotions of hurt and pain back to you again and again. That is the time for you to say emphatically, "In Jesus' name, I know He took my pain on the cross." As you declare the truth, the emotions of hurt feelings will dissipate as you focus on Jesus your healer instead of on the pain. In the same way that the sound from the big church bell rings loudly at first and then less and less, the memories of hurt will become less and less as you declare the truth that Jesus has healed you. In a very short time, you will get to the place where the devil cannot even tempt you anymore in this area. You will be completely and totally healed.

REFLECTION
After the first step of forgiving those who hurt us, write down the next steps for healing as mentioned above.

1, ask God to forgive them
2, ask God to forgive our attitudes + sin
3, Confess our sins one to another
4. ask someone to lay hands on me
   & pray for me,

Free to have a sound mind

We live in a day of extreme stress. Many of us face mental anguish. Jesus came to set us free from this curse on our minds that has its root based in unwholesome fear. The scriptures tell us in 2 Timothy 1:7, *For God has not given us a spirit of fear, but of power and of love and of a sound mind (NKJ).*

God's purpose for your life is for you to have a sound mind. Perhaps your ancestors had some type of mental problems. God says that you can be free from that curse in Jesus' name. As I was growing up, I can vividly remember various members of my extended family who had a history of mental illness. I feared that I would spend periods of my life mentally ill in a mental hospital like some of my family members. One day I came to the realization that I didn't have to fear mental illness because Jesus Christ became a curse for me. By the grace of God, I have been freed from that curse in Jesus' name.

The Lord's will for each of us is to have peace of mind. Isaiah 26:3 says, *You will keep in perfect peace him whose mind is steadfast, because he trusts in you.*

Since I have been set free from the curse in Jesus' name, the Lord has delivered me from the fear of mental illness. We serve a good God! We can trust Him! He has promised us perfect peace as we continue to focus on our heavenly Father, the author of all peace (1 Corinthians 14:33).

You and I are in a brand new family, the family of God, through faith in Jesus Christ. We have a brand new household, the household of God. Our new Father in heaven does not have any mental problems at all.

We need to break every curse that is over our lives in Jesus' name. By the grace of God, I have broken every curse over my life in the name of Jesus. I am a free man! Today is your day of freedom. Today is the day for any curse over your life to be completely broken in Jesus' name.

REFLECTION
If you are fearful, stressed out and worried all the time, 2 Timothy 1:7 gives the solution. What is it?
To claim his gift of empowerment + liberty.

CHAPTER 4

You Can Be Completely Free

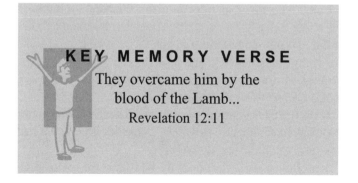

KEY MEMORY VERSE

They overcame him by the
blood of the Lamb...
Revelation 12:11

Financial freedom

To summarize the previous section, we learned we are redeemed from the curse in every facet of our existence. The curse is still in the world, but it has no right to be on us as Christians. We are redeemed from the curse! The curse on our spiritual, physical, emotional and mental lives is removed by the blood of Jesus.

A fifth area of freedom we can experience is financial freedom. 2 Corinthians 8:9 says, *For you know the grace of our Lord Jesus Christ, that though he was rich, yet for your sakes he became poor, so that you through his poverty might become rich.* God wants to prosper us in every way, including financially, so we can give financially in order for the good news of Jesus to be taken throughout the whole world. Some people think it is godly to be poor. What they don't understand is that poverty is a part of the curse. If poverty is godly, then we should never be giving money to the poor. We would be hindering them from living in this godly state!

If you are struggling financially right now, I have good news for you. You don't have to be poor. God wants to prosper you. God wants to bless you and give you hope. Some people think that money is the root of evil. That's not exactly what the scripture says in I Timothy 6:10. It says that the *love* of money is a root of evil. If we love money more than God, it is idolatry and leads us away from God.

It is wise to remember that prosperity and material things can never make us happy. Only Jesus can give us fulfillment and the abundant life. At the same time, the Lord desires to bless us. God wants to prosper us so we can give to our families, the church, the poor, and give to see His kingdom built throughout the whole world.

A lady who was experiencing deep financial problems in her home, came to her pastor for help. Both her husband and her son were out of work. The pastor told her, "You need to read Galatians 3:13." He opened his Bible and read it to her, *Christ redeemed us from the curse of the law by becoming a curse for us, for it is written: "Cursed is everyone who is hung on a tree."*

"Jesus Christ became a curse for you," he explained to her, "so that you can be financially free." She came day after day for advice and counsel but didn't really listen.

Then about a year after she had first sought the pastor's advice, she came into his office and met with him once again. She said,

"Guess what happened? I am finally prosperous. I was reading the Bible one day and I received a revelation from God." She said, "It's Galatians 3:13." (This was the same truth that the pastor had been telling her over and over again, but this time she herself received a revelation from God.) She said, "Here's what happened. I realized God wanted to prosper me. This poverty was a curse over my life. So, I went and got a job at a restaurant. The joy of the Lord was in my life, and I knew the financial curse had been broken. Later I bought the restaurant." She is a prosperous woman today, because the favor of God is on her. In fact, people come back just because of the godly atmosphere in her restaurant. The scriptures tell us in Ephesians 4:28, *He who has been stealing must steal no longer, but must work, doing something useful with his own hands, that he may have something to share with those in need.*

REFLECTION
*Is it godly to be poor?
Who does God want to
use to spread the gospel
and meet the needs of
millions in the world?*

Jesus wants to bless us so we can give to others. As we work with an attitude of freedom and joy, we will experience the Lord's blessing. The curse has been broken. The Lord desires to prosper you as you obey Him.

It's not Godly nor is it UnGodly it is just a financial position. I don't Know, but the reason why you are poor may be ungodly.

Social freedom

TME

A sixth area of freedom from the curse is social freedom. God wants us to have good success in every realm and area of our life, including the way in which we relate to people socially. When I was growing up, I had a hard time looking people in the eye because I felt inferior. It was a curse that had to be broken. Today, by the grace of God, I love to meet people. The curse of being afraid to face people is gone in Jesus' name! According to the Bible, being afraid of people is a trap! But when we really trust the Lord, we can find safety in our relationships. *Fear of man will prove to be a snare, but whoever trusts in the Lord is kept safe (Proverbs 29:25).*

Jesus had great favor with the people of His day. Wherever Jesus went, "the common people heard Him gladly" (Mark 12:37 NKJ). I believe Jesus was really fun to be with. Children loved to be with Jesus (Matthew 18:2-5).

God wants you and me to be able to relate to other people in a positive way. A curse that may be over you from generations past will hinder you from relating to people in a sociable and loving way. Jesus has liberated us from that horrible harvest of sin that can affect generations. That curse needs to be broken today in the name of Jesus. Jesus Christ became a curse for you!

This does not mean that we will escape persecution or that everyone will like us. Persecution may take many forms. In some countries today, Christians are tortured and imprisoned for their beliefs. I was recently in such a nation, meeting with Christian leaders, most of whom had been in prison for their faith. Other times, Christians may be deprived of a job for which they are eligible or held up to ridicule at work or school, all because of their religious persuasion. 2 Timothy 3:12 tells us we will all experience some kind of persecution if we truly live godly lives. *In fact, everyone who wants to live a godly life in Christ Jesus will be persecuted.*

Jesus instructed us to rejoice when others say all kinds of evil against us falsely for His sake (Matthew 5:11-12), and yet, the Bible tells us that people in the early church had favor with all the people, and people were coming to know Jesus Christ every day (Acts 2:47). Are you finding God's favor on your life? The Lord's desire is for you to experience the favor of the Lord. Take a close look at Psalms 5:12, *For surely, O Lord, you bless the righteous; you surround them with your favor as with a shield.*

REFLECTION
A social snare is what, according to Proverbs 29:25? What does Psalms 5:12 say God wants to surround us with?

God desires to surround you with His favor today. Declare your freedom from the curse through Jesus Christ. The price of redemption is paid. Receive it for yourself. Today is your day of freedom.

Freedom from demonic activity

DAY 3

A seventh area of freedom is freedom from demonic activity. The word "demon possessed" in New Testament Greek is the word *demonized* which means *to have a demon*. People throughout the New Testament often suffered from Satan's oppression and influence because of an indwelling evil spirit. Jesus and the New Testament Christians were constantly casting demons out of people. *When evening came, many who were demon-possessed were brought to him, and he drove out the spirits with a word and healed all the sick (Matthew 8:16).*

✱ Fear of man
✱ His favor

In our modern society, people often are too sophisticated to believe that individuals can have demons. Some people don't even believe in demons. The Bible tells us, however, that demons are evil spirit beings who are enemies of God and humans (Matthew 12:43-45). In addition, they can live in the bodies of unbelievers to enslave them to immorality and evil (Mark 5:15; Luke 4:41; 8:27-28; Acts 16:18) and they can cause physical illness (Matthew 4:24; Luke 5:12-13) although not all illness is the result of evil spirits.

Whether people want to believe it or not, the truth is, many people today are tormented by demons. Those involved in magic or spiritism using Ouija boards, seances, tarot cards, or horoscopes are dealing with evil spirits and can be led into demonic bondage. Demonic activity in their lives may express itself in fits of anger, confusion, violence, immorality, depression...the list goes on and on.

People sometimes ask me if Christians can have demonic activity in their lives. Yes, they can, but it doesn't mean that they are demon possessed or under the complete control of a demon. However, demons may have influence in Christians thoughts and emotions and actions when they fail to submit to the Holy Spirit's leading in their lives.

I was speaking to a Christian leader who told me he had a demon of anger cast out of his life. He had gone through times of uncontrollable anger and didn't understand why. Finally one day, he confided in a pastor who took authority over the demon and cast it out in Jesus' name. He has not been the same since. Today he is one of the most gentle men I have ever met. Jesus Christ set him free.

Although Satan constantly wars against God's people, trying to draw them away from their loyalty to Christ, Jesus promised believers authority over the power of Satan and his demons. He became a curse for us so that we can be free from any type of demon spirit influencing our lives. We do not have to fear the powers of darkness. Years ago, a man in a backslidden state came to me and said, "Larry, I want you to know that I have used a voodoo doll and have placed a curse on you." There was no fear in my heart when he said that. Do you know why? Because I knew that Jesus Christ became a curse for me. A curse could not be placed on me, because I was protected by the blood of Jesus Christ. *They overcame him by the blood of the Lamb...(Revelation 12:11).*

As Christians, we live by faith in the Word of God. We are living under His grace and are protected with God's law of protection from the enemy through Christ! As Christians, we have power over Satan because of what Jesus did on the cross. He shattered the power of Satan's realm when he died and rose again. He disarmed Satan.

The Bible says, *For God has not given us a spirit of fear... (2 Timothy 1:7 NKJ)*. If we have a paralyzing fear of Satan and his evil intentions, we are not just fearful; we have a spirit of fear. A spirit of fear can be a demonic spirit of deception. Satan is the author of fear and wants us to walk in fear. Demonic spirits of all kinds must be resisted and commanded to leave

REFLECTION
What does it mean to be demonized? What sets us free, according to Revelation 12:11?

+ to have a demon
+ blood of Christ.

in Jesus' name. We can break the power they attempt to exert over us. If we are dealing with a violent temper, depression, a sudden compulsion to commit suicide, or other life-dominating problem, these very well may be demonic spirits that are controlling our lives. We cannot be oblivious to their deception. We must be alert to Satan's schemes and temptations and desire to be set free.

Resist the devil, and he will flee

To be set free from demonic bondage we must resist the devil by prayer and proclaim God's Word as we call upon the mighty name of Jesus. A friend told me he once sensed a strange, evil presence at a friend's house. Calling upon the name of Jesus Christ, a few Christian believers prayed and took authority over a curse that needed to be broken over that home. The evil presence left. James 4:7 says, *Submit yourselves, then, to God. Resist the devil, and he will flee from you.*

Smith Wigglesworth was an evangelist in Great Britain years ago. He compared the devil to a stray dog that is barking at our heels. He taught that unless we resist the dog, he will continue with his "yelping" and aggravation. But if we boldly tell him to leave us alone, he will flee. The devil has no choice when we resist him in Jesus' name. He must flee.

As Christians, we can call upon Jesus to defeat Satan and his demonic powers. Matthew 12:29-30 says we can tie up the strong man (Satan) and rob his house (set free those who are enslaved to Satan). *Or again, how can anyone enter a strong man's house and*

DAY 4

carry off his possessions unless he first ties up the strong man? Then he can rob his house (Matthew 12:29-30).

We can drive demons out in the name of Jesus by "tying up" the demonic spirit that is influencing our lives or someone else's life. Only then can we be free. As believers, we can provide deliverance for those who have been held captive by Satan's power. *And these signs will accompany those who believe: In my name they will drive out demons; they will speak in new tongues (Mark 16:17).*

Casting out demons is a ministry that the Lord has given to those who believe in Him. Christians are called to minister deliverance to those bound by Satan. If you believe the Lord is calling you to set people free from demon spirits, I encourage you to follow the example of Jesus. Jesus sent His disciples out two by two to minister, and they came back excited! Why? *...Even the demons submit to us in your name!"* they said (Luke 10:17).

We should note that Jesus gives His disciples a word of caution, *...do not rejoice that the spirits submit to you, but rejoice that your names are written in heaven" (v. 20).* Jesus cautioned the disciples to not make the power over the demons the source of their joy but rejoice because of their relationship with Him.

REFLECTION
What two things must we do to make the devil flee?
How do we defeat demonic powers, according to Matthew 12:29-30?

The fact remained—demons could not stand in the presence of the disciples who were commissioned ＊Submit to God, resist the opposer. by Jesus to cast them out. The Lord ＊By binding Satan & his demons has also commissioned us to cast demons out of people and be set From influencing free from demonic activity in our own lives in Jesus' powerful our lives name!

Renounce demonic spirits

DAY 5

Sometimes people get involved innocently with the demonic by dabbling in paranormal energies in order to gain knowledge of the future or uncover secrets—reading tarot cards, demonic games like Dungeons and Dragons and the ouija board, water witching, seances

Occult practices
Leviticus 19:31; 20:6
Deuteronomy 18:10-11
Revelation 9:21

to contact the dead, use of drugs to produce "spiritual experiences"—all these kinds of practices are associated with the occult. Attempting to communicate with the supernatural through these kinds of methods is actually communication with demons (1 Samuel 28:8-14; 2 Kings 21:6; Isaiah 8:19).

Getting involved in these kind of occult practices are dangerous and can lead to demonic bondage. The Bible gives these warnings:

...Do not practice divination or sorcery (Leviticus 19:26).

Do not turn to mediums or seek out spiritists, for you will be defiled by them. I am the Lord your God (Leviticus 19:31).

As a young boy, I participated in a type of *divination* by trying to "smell for water" on our family farm. We believed that by holding a rod, we could locate underground streams of water, thus knowing where to drill a well. Although I was completely unaware of it at the time, I was dabbling in the occult. Trying to uncover the unknown forces of nature by using superstitious practices like this is really opening ourselves to demonic spirits. After I received Jesus Christ as Lord, I claimed my freedom from the curse the enemy tried to place over my life through my involvement in this occult practice. Years ago, I also played with an ouija board, a game that attempts to uncover secret things by submitting to unknown spiritual forces. Again, I broke that curse over my life in the name of Jesus Christ.

There are two supernatural powers—the power of God through Jesus Christ, and the power of the enemy. A curse can be placed over our lives if we are involved in any type of occult practices. I have ministered to people who had an intense desire to commit suicide or fell into depression because the devil held them in bondage due to their involvement in the occult. The good news is this! You can be set completely free. If you or your ancestors have been involved in any type of occult activity, you can be set free. When you renounce those demonic spirits in the name of Jesus, the demons can no longer have any control of your life.

A friend of ours had migraine headaches for more than eight years. In her case, this physical ailment was

REFLECTION
What dangers must we be aware of when someone is involved in the supernatural? How do occult practices affec the lives of those involved?

✝ it can lead to demonic bondage. ✝ cu

tied into her involvement in the occult. In desperation, she went to some Christians for help. They rebuked the devil in Jesus' name, and she was set free from the curse of constant headaches over her life.

Our lives are like an onion with many layers of skin. Maybe you have been set free from demonic spirits in your life. There may be

✝ It curses us, depression, suicide, sickness

44   *Biblical Foundations*

little layers that God has already peeled off. However, the Lord may take you through other areas of freedom in the future.

He loves us and takes us step by step. He knows what we can handle. As the Lord reveals other areas of bondage in our lives, we receive His freedom. Then another layer comes off. The Lord continues this process until we are completely clean and are the people God has called us to be. He is committed to seeing us set completely free. This process may take days, months, or even years.

Free from family curses

Earlier in this book (Chapter 1, Day 6 and Chapter 2, Day 3) we mentioned generational (family) curses that may be passed down through the generations. Unrepented sin can leave a spiritual weakness toward a particular sin in a family line. For example, a sexual sin may produce a curse. The curse then causes a generational weakness to that sin to be passed down in the family line. If the sin is not made right before God, it continues its pattern and strongly influences our lives.

Generational sins cause spiritual *strongholds* or thinking in our minds that cause us to say, "Even God cannot change this circumstance in my life. It's hopeless." We begin to accept this lie and fall into sin that produces a stronghold in our lives. There are multitudes of strongholds that can be passed through family lines: addictions like alcohol, food, compulsive spending; mental problems like depression, rage, worry; sexual problems like homosexuality, fornication, pornography; heart issues that include bitterness, greed, rebellion, legalism, gossip.

First, it is important to identify the strongholds that afflict our family lines because we can demolish these strongholds in our lives. *The weapons we fight with are not the weapons of the world. On the contrary, they have divine power to demolish strongholds. We demolish arguments and every pretension that sets itself up against the knowledge of God, and we take captive every thought to make it obedient to Christ (2 Corinthians 10:4-5).*

Next, we should repent of our own sin. Even though we have inherited a spiritual weakness to a particular sin in our family, it is

REFLECTION
Identify any generational sins in your family line. Write them down and walk through the steps of repentance and forgiveness mentioned above.

† Financial, anger, drunkeness, & mental illness, wastefullness, gluttony, sexual...ete...

no excuse for the sin we have committed. Then, we forgive our ancestors for bringing the sin into the family line. *If you forgive anyone his sins, they are forgiven; if you do not forgive them, they are not forgiven (John 20:23).* We cannot have unforgiveness in our hearts. Finally, we need to repent of (or renounce) the sin. By doing so, we break the power of that sin in our generation. We remove Satan's legal right to continue plaguing us and our children in that particular area.

Our spiritual weapons

As Christians, we are engaged in a spiritual conflict with evil. Although we have been guaranteed victory through Christ's death on the cross, we must wage a spiritual warfare by the power of the Holy Spirit using our spiritual armor (Ephesians 6:10-18). For more on spiritual warfare, see Biblical Foundation 12, Chapter 2.

One time, the disciples could not cast out a demon in a young boy, and Jesus said...*this kind can come out only by prayer ["and fasting," in some translations] (Mark 9:29).*

Jesus implied that if His disciples had maintained a life of prayer, like He did, they could have successfully cast this demon out. When we recognize we are in conflict against spiritual forces and powers of evil, we will live fervently before God and be equipped by faith to see others delivered from demonic spirits.

To overcome evil, God has given us weapons. The first weapon is the "name of Jesus Christ." The scriptures tell us, *That at the name of Jesus every knee should bow, in heaven and on earth and under the earth, and every tongue confess that Jesus Christ is Lord, to the glory of God the Father (Philippians 2:10-11).*

Some time ago, I was awakened in the night and sensed an evil presence in my room. I was away from home, and no one else was in the house where I was staying. I felt like I was frozen to my bed. I could only call out the name of "Jesus." The evil presence left and I was able to go back to sleep. There is power in the name of Jesus.

The second weapon the Lord has given to us against the enemy is the "blood of Jesus Christ." I have actually witnessed demons in people who have shrieked in fear at the mention of the blood of Jesus. On one occasion, a man with demons held his hands over his ears and screamed when the blood of Jesus was mentioned. The blood of the Lamb has freed us from the power of the enemy. The scriptures tell us in Revelation 12:11, *they overcame him by the blood of the Lamb and by the word of their testimony; they did not love their lives so much as to shrink from death (Revelation 12:11).*

The third weapon the Lord has given to us against the curse of the enemy is the "word of our testimony." Our testimony is simply confessing what the Lord has done in our lives and what God is saying about us. We know what God says about us by believing His Word. The truth of God's Word sets us free.

In closing, I am going to ask you to pray the following prayer aloud. We will confess the Word of God and our testimony, and find freedom from the curse in Jesus' name.

"In the name of Jesus Christ, I renounce any involvement that I or my family has ever had with the occult back to the third and fourth generation in Jesus' name. I declare that I am a child of the living God through faith in Jesus Christ. Jesus Christ is the Lord and King of my life. His blood has cleansed me from every sin and from every curse that the enemy would have tried to place against my life. The Bible says, 'whom the Son sets free is free indeed' (John 8:36). I am free today in the mighty name of Jesus. I declare my freedom from spiritual bondage and false guilt in Jesus' Name. I declare freedom today from any type of physical illness or disease in the name of Jesus. I declare I am emotionally whole in the name of Jesus Christ. I forgive anyone who has ever hurt me in Jesus' name. I declare that I am free mentally in the name of Jesus. I declare that I am free financially, and I shall prosper in Jesus' name. I declare in the name of Jesus that I am free socially, and the favor of God is on my life. I declare that I am free from every demonic stronghold and strategy of the enemy in the name of Jesus. The strong man has been bound in Jesus' name and Jesus Christ has set

REFLECTION
Name the three spiritual weapons explained here. How powerful is your testimony against demonic powers?

me free. I declare the blood of Jesus Christ has set me free! I claim my inheritance according to the Word of God that Jesus Christ has become a curse for me. I thank you for it in Jesus' name. Amen."

If you feel you need to have another person pray with you and take authority over any demonic spirit or influence in your life, do it! He will be faithful to lead you to the right person. This Spirit-filled believer in Jesus Christ who has an intimate relationship with Jesus can pray for you, and the Lord will set you free.

* prayer, fasting, name of Jesus
blood of Jesus, word of our testimony

* Very

What is a Curse?

1. **Sin enters a perfect world and changes it forever**
   a. Sin entered the world through the disobedience of Adam and Eve (Romans 5:12).
   b. Hence we live in a fallen or cursed world and humans are born with an impulse toward sin and selfishness. Romans 8:5-8

2. **Satan now causes havoc in the world**
   a. Even the ground is cursed (Genesis 3:17) and sin and its curse began to increase in the world.
   b. We see the results in the misery people experience in the world. Satan continues to cause havoc in the world as a result of the initial curse.

3. **Jesus reigns over the devil**
   a. Although Satan controls this present age because the world is in rebellion against God's rule, Jesus came to destroy his work (1 John 3:8).
   b. Jesus came to establish God's kingdom in our hearts and deliver us from Satan's dominion.
   c. Jesus reigns over the devil (John 14:30; 1 John 4:4).

4. **Jesus became a curse for us**
   a. Because of what Jesus did on the cross, we can be free of the devil's lies over our lives. Jesus became a curse for us. Galatians 3:13
   b. Jesus redeemed us or bought us back.
      Ex: Boy buys back his boat after he lost it.
   c. We have been bought back from the curse over our lives (of breaking God's law—sin).

5. People suffer because our planet was turned over to the powers of darkness

a. There is a curse on this world ever since sin entered. Both believers and nonbelievers experience suffering as an ongoing consequence of the fall of Adam and Eve. We now live on a planet that was turned over to the powers of darkness.

Ex: Cancer and other diseases may be the result of an unhealthy diet or from ingesting food loaded with pesticides, etc.

b. God never intended for evil to be a part of His plan. He does not cause evil to happen to us (James 1:13).

6. People suffer because humans make wrong choices

a. A law in the universe set up by God is called "sowing and reaping" (Galatians 6:7). We will reap the consequences of wrong choices.

b. Sins of parents can follow children through generations (Exodus 20:5; Deuteronomy 5:9) but this generational curse can be broken.

c. We must avoid whatever removes us from God's protection—confess known sin in our lives. But sometimes we make bad choices innocently and God may allow hardships as a means of discipline (Hebrews 12:5-6).

7. People suffer because of direct satanic attack

a. Demonic curses are placed on people so they are crippled emotionally, spiritually or physically.

b. Believers are not immune to Satan's attacks, but "a curse without a cause cannot alight." Direct attack occurs because:

(1) we are not walking under Christ's protection and open ourselves up to demonic attack

(2) in the case of Paul, the Lord allowed Satan access to him so he would not become proud (2 Corinthians 12:7).

We Can Reclaim What the Enemy Stole

1. We can be victorious!

a. As Christians, we can have victory in every areas of our lives! Jesus came to deliver us from Satan's dominion (Genesis 3:14-15) and establish God's kingdom in our hearts.

b. Tragedies in our lives do not originate with God (James 1:17). The Lord provides a way out of our bondage to sin and suffering. His plan for our lives is one of hope. Jeremiah 29:11

2. We live in a covenant relationship with God

a. In the Old Testament covenant, God promises to bind Himself to His faithful people to be their God. In the New Testament, God made a new covenant with us in Jesus Christ—a promise to bestow divine protection and blessing on those who, through faith, accept Jesus and receive His promises (Galatians 3:6-9).

b. A covenant depends on our obedience to God. If we obey, we are blessed, if not, we are cursed. Deuteronomy 28:1-3; 15

c. It is not God's will for suffering to come upon our lives. Suffering is part of the original curse, and God wants us to be free.

3. We cannot allow the enemy to lie to us

a. The devil has lied to many Christians (John 8:44) telling them they cannot be free of bondages in their lives.

b. When you were born again, you received a new Father. He is not under the curse. He can set you free from every curse. That's why He went to the cross, so all our insecurities, fears, curses can be broken.

c. God wants to give us good gifts (James 1:17).

4. We must stake our claim!

a. Adam's sin brought death, but Christ brought grace and life. Romans 5:15; 19

b. Christ reclaimed what Satan tried to take from us. We must take back areas of our lives the devil has stolen.

   Ex: Israelites had to go into the promised land, step by step, to claim it (Joshua 1:3).

c. Legally, as a Christian, you are entitled to peace, joy, good health, etc. but if the devil has stolen it from you, you can claim back those areas.

5. We apply God's Word to our lives

a. We are delivered from the power of darkness and are now in Christ's kingdom (Colossians 1:13).

b. We can reign in life (Romans 5:17) and experience wholeness.

c. The Word of God must be applied to our lives. As we confess its truth, faith is built in our hearts (Romans 10:17) and we can overcome life-dominating patterns in our lives or any other trial.

6. We guard our tongues

a. Words are powerful (Matthew 12:34; Matthew 12:36-37).

b. By our words, we can pronounce either a blessing or curse on our lives.

c. The thing we fear may come upon us (Job 3:25) but God has not given us a spirit of fear (2 Timothy 1:7).

d. Speak life-giving words that release hope.

7. We release our inheritance

a. We are God's children through faith in Jesus. Romans 8:16

b. Spiritually, we must receive our inheritance in order to be set free of bondages in our lives.

   Ex: Before you receive an inheritance, you must sign the will to release it.

Receiving Freedom in Jesus' Name

1. Free spiritually!

a. One area of freedom from the curse is *spiritual freedom.* 1 John 1:9

b. The devil may try to tell us we are not saved, but he is a liar. Romans 8:1-2

c. The curse of false guilt tries to push us into depression, etc. and it must be broken in Jesus' name.

Ex: Farmer battling false guilt drives a stake in ground and confesses his freedom.

2. Free from sickness and disease

a. Jesus carried our diseases on the cross.
Matthew 8:16-17; Isaiah 53:4-5
It is God's will that we are healed and healthy.

b. Every sickness has been hung on the cross through Jesus Christ.

c. Seek the presence of Jesus and saturate yourself with God's Word and expect a miracle (Matthew 7:8;19:26).

3. Hindrances to healing

a. Hindrances to healing may be unconfessed sin, demonic oppression, fear, past disappointments that undermine present faith, unbiblical teaching, failure of leaders to pray the prayer of faith, unbelief, self-centered behavior. Sometimes the reason is not apparent.

b. Don't give up if prayers for healing are not answered (Philippians 4:4). God's purposes are for our greater good and we cannot always understand.

c. We choose to live by what God's Word says even if we do not see the expected results.

4. Free from painful memories
   a. God wants us to be healed emotionally (Luke 4:18-19).
   b. We can break free from the curse of painful memories from the past.
   Ex: How a young man forgave his dad and was healed.

5. Forgive, forgive, forgive
   a. A key to being healed is to forgive those who have hurt us. Matthew 6:14-15
   b. Matthew 18-Parable of a servant owing money. If we don't forgive those who have hurt us, we may be tormented. Matthew 18:34-35

6. And forgive some more!
   a. We not only forgive those who have hurt us, but ask God to forgive them.
   b. We should also ask God to forgive us for any attempt to hide our sin (Proverbs 28:13).
   c. Confess your faults to someone and have him pray for you. James 5:16

7. Free to have a sound mind
   a. Jesus came to set us free from this curse based on unwholesome fear (2 Timothy 1:7).
   b. God's will is for us to have peace of mind (Isaiah 26:3).

You Can Be Completely Free

1. Financial freedom
a. God wants us to prosper (2 Corinthians 8:9).

Ex: Woman finally realizes Christ redeemed her from the curse of financial problems (Galatians 3:13).

b. Jesus wants to bless us so we can give to others. E p h - esians 4:28

2. Social freedom
a. Feeling inferior is a curse (Proverbs 29:25).

b. Christians should live joyful lives. The early Christians "had favor" with the people around them (Acts 2:47).

c. However, this does not mean Christians will escape ridicule or persecution for living godly lives (2 Timothy 3:12).

d. We need to experience the favor of the Lord and walk in social freedom (Psalms 5:12).

3. Freedom from demonic activity
a. People today are tormented by demons and Jesus can heal them just as in biblical times (Matthew 8:16).

b. Demonic activity may express itself in fits of anger, confusion, immorality, depression, violence, etc.

Ex: Christian leader had a demon of anger cast out of his life.

4. Resist the devil, and he will flee
a. We resist the devil by prayer, proclaiming God's Word and taking authority over him (James 4:7).

b. We can drive demons out and set free those who are enslaved (Matthew 12:29-30).

5. Renounce demonic spirits

a. Getting involved in any kind of occult practice is dangerous (tarot cards, ouija board game, water witching, seances, etc.) and can lead to demonic bondage (Leviticus 19:26, 31).

b. Renounce any kind of demonic activity in which you participated and be set free in Jesus' name!

6. Free from family curses

a. Unrepented sin may leave a spiritual weakness toward a particular sin which follows a family line.

   Ex: A sexual sin may produce a curse which causes a generational weakness (stronghold) to that sin to be passed down in the family line.

b. Identify the stronghold so it can be demolished.
   2 Corinthians 10:4-5

c. We also need to repent of our own sin, forgive our ancestors (John 20:23), and renounce the sin to break its power in our generation.

7. Our spiritual weapons

a. We wage spiritual warfare against evil using our spiritual armor (Ephesians 6:10-18).

b. A weapon to overcome evil: the name of Jesus.
   Philippians 2:10-11

c. Two more weapons against the enemy: the blood of Jesus Christ and the word of our testimony (Revelation 12:11).

d. Pray and take authority over any demonic influence in your life and find freedom in Jesus' name.

Chapter 1
What is a Curse?
Journaling space for reflection questions

DAY 1 *How did sin curse this world (Romans 5:12)?*
What does our sinful nature cause us to do?

DAY 2 *Why was the ground cursed in Genesis 3:17?*
What happened as a result (Romans 6:23)?

DAY 3 *Why did Jesus come, according to 1 John 3:8?*
How does Jesus destroy the works of the devil in our lives?

How can we be free of the curse of the law (Galatians 3:13)?
What does it mean to be redeemed?

 In light of the suffering caused by Satan on this earth, what is
our responsibility as Christians?

How do our choices make a difference in the way our lives are
lived? Is it possible to be affected by the sins of our ancestors?

 Are believers immune to Satan's attacks?
How can we be alert to Satan's schemes (1 Peter 5:8-10)?

Chapter 2
We Can Reclaim What the Enemy Stole
Journaling space for reflection questions

What is Satan's fate (Genesis 3:14-15)? What is God's plan for our lives (Jeremiah 29:11)?

What does our covenant with Jesus Christ depend upon? Name some areas that are a part of the original curse. How can we be set free?

Has the devil lied to you about an area of your life in which you do not seem to have victory? What can you do about it?

What does the Lord promise to those who want to reclaim what Satan has taken from them (Joshua 1:3)?

God's Word is likened to what offensive weapon (Ephesians 6:17)? How can we attack the powers of darkness and put them to flight (Romans 10:17)?

How can the words you say condemn you? Give examples from your life.

When we realize what our inheritance is, how do we release it? Speak Philippians 4:13 aloud.

Chapter 3
Receiving Freedom in Jesus' Name
Journaling space for reflection questions

How do you get rid of feelings of guilt and condemnation (Romans 8:1-2)? What is the difference between conviction and condemnation?

Put your name in place of the words "our" and "we" in 1 Peter 2:24. Do you believe God wants you to be free of every sickness and disease?

As an heir of all the promises in the Bible, why wouldn't you want to take all you can have? What should you do if your prayers for healing are not answered (Philippians 4:4)?

Do you have painful memories of past hurts?
Why do you think you are unable to break free?

What is the first step in receiving healing of memories (Matthew 6:14-15)? What happens if we do not forgive (Matthew 18:34-35)?

After the first step of forgiving those who hurt us, write down the next steps for healing as mentioned above.

If you are fearful, stressed out and worried all the time, 2 Timothy 1:7 gives the solution. What is it?

Chapter 4
You Can Be Completely Free
Journaling space for reflection questions

DAY 1

Is it godly to be poor? Who does God want to use to spread the gospel and meet the needs of millions in the world?

DAY 2

A social snare is what, according to Proverbs 29:25? What does Psalms 5:12 say God wants to surround us with?

DAY 3

What does it mean to be demonized? What sets us free, according to Revelation 12:11?

DAY 4

What two things must we do to make the devil flee? How do we defeat demonic powers, according to Matthew 12:29-30?

DAY 5

What dangers must we be aware of when someone is involved in the supernatural? How do occult practices affect the lives of those involved?

DAY 6

Identify any generational sins in your family line. Write them down and walk through the steps of repentance and forgiveness mentioned above.

DAY 7

Name the three spiritual weapons explained here. How powerful is your testimony against demonic powers?

Daily Devotional Extra Days

If you are using this book as a daily devotional, you will notice there are 28 days in this study. Depending on the month, you may need the three extra days' studies given here.

Make Me Clean!

DAY 29

Read Mark 1:40-42. Put yourself in the place of the leper in this story. Ask Jesus to help you with any curse or bondage in your life. What is compassion?
Repeat aloud what Jesus said to the leper in verse 41.

Healed and Set Free

DAY 30

Read Mark 2:3-12. Whose faith did Jesus see in verse 5? How did Jesus react to this faith? What did Jesus see in the hearts of the scribes (verse 8)? How did Jesus react to them? What does this teach us about the motives of the heart?

Free from Bondage

DAY 31

Read Mark 3:3-5,10-15. Did the man with the withered hand ask Jesus to heal him? What does this say about the compassion of Jesus? Read verse 11 again. Why do demons know Jesus? What does Jesus tell them to do? In verse 15, is this power Jesus gave to the disciples the very same power He used against the demons? Are you free from every curse and bondage that may have been placed over your life?